...lly has the novel it

is rich in documentation

of note to come out of

that earth-shattering eruption. And fine fiction it is, melding Jon Gosch's taut, fresh style with an unforgettable cast and a riveting plot that gathers with all the tension and inexorability of the very eruption itself."

—Robert Michael Pyle, 2x Washington State Book Award winner and author of *Wintergreen* and *Where Bigfoot Walks*

"*Deep Fire Rise* perfectly captures the world of Mount St. Helens at its most terrifying moment. A magnificent read."

—Terry Trueman, Printz Honor Author of *Stuck in Neutral*

"*Deep Fire Rise* is a murder mystery, a character study, and a depiction of place that builds in tension like a swelling volcano. Having covered the eruption of Mount St. Helens as a journalist and ridden with Clark County deputies, I can testify just how impressively Jon Gosch has captured that time and culture."

—William Dietrich, Pulitzer Prize-winning journalist and *NY Times* bestselling author of the Ethan Gage adventure series

"Jon Gosch's *Deep Fire Rise* rings with authenticity. The intimate, complicated, and downright strange relationships amongst the people in these small towns are pitch perfect, as is the music of the dialogue and rhythms of the prose."

—Bruce Holbert, 2015 Washington State Book Award-winning author of *The Hour of Lead*

"A bright young talent is on display in this vivid, avant-garde take on our local lore."

—Michael Gurian, *NY Times* bestselling author of *The Wonder of Boys*

DEEP

FIRE

RISE

Also by Jon Gosch

If We Get There

JON GOSCH

DEEP FIRE RISE

Latah Books
Spokane, Washington

Book design by Gray Dog Press and Andrew Juarez

Cover photo by Murray Foubister
under Creative Commons Attribution-Share Alike 2.0 Generic license

ISBN-13: 978-0-9997075-0-0
Library of Congress Control Number: 2017918618
Cataloging-in-Publication Data is available upon request

Manufactured in the United States of America

Production by Gray Dog Press
www.GrayDogPress.com

Published by Latah Books
331 W Main, Spokane, WA 99201
www.latahbooks.com

Author may be contacted at jongosch@hotmail.com

for Tim Gosch, Vern Gosch,
and Andrew Hamilton

I

I'd been working for my father-in-law at the gas station in Toutle for a few months when Mount St. Helens started rumbling. It went from being the most boring job I ever had to the most interesting in about a day and a half. As soon as word got out that there might be an eruption, people started pouring in from all over the country. From all over the world. I couldn't believe the sorts of folks that showed up. Some real kooks. But even so, this guy stood out.

I believe it was the second week of May when he came through the store. He walked up to the counter with a basket full of junk food and said he needed a map. I asked him which kind of a map he was looking for and he said, I'm looking for a map to Hell.

It's not too hard to remember a guy who says something as strange as that. But I knew what he meant. Like a lot of people at the time, he was after one of those maps that showed you how to get around the roadblocks and drive right up to the volcano on the logging roads. Bootleg maps. I'm still not entirely sure if they were legal.

Well, I can be a wise guy sometimes so I told him that if he was looking for a map to Hell then any of the ordinary ones would do. They all show you how to get to

Tacoma. He didn't think that was funny. He just sorta stared at me so I pulled one of the bootleg maps out from under the counter and started ringing him up.

While I was bagging his stuff, I asked him what he was planning to do out there on those logging roads. Was he trying to get right up next to the volcano? He shook his head. Not next to it, he told me. He wanted to look inside the volcano.

Inside.

He'd murdered those folks and now he wanted to get a glimpse of what Hell would look like. Honestly, I can't say that I blame him. I did two tours of Vietnam so I've been there myself. Though it never quite drove me up the slopes of a smoking volcano.

As he was walking back to his vehicle I had Dolly take over the cash register so I could follow him outside. He was loading up his things when I began to feel the ground trembling and heard what sounded like thunder way off in the distance. But it wasn't thunder. It was that mountain. And before long it commenced to spew ash about a mile up into the air. Soon enough the sun was blotted out and the sky looked as black and ominous as the very end of days.

We both stood there watching it for a good long while and then he finally turned around and noticed me standing there. And that's when he smiled at me. Gave me the craziest grin I ever saw in my whole life. And then he got in his vehicle and took off screeching down the highway. Straight toward all that darkness and ash.

I still don't quite know what his hurry was. And I'm also not certain if he ever did get to peer down into that volcano. But it sure did seem like he was on his way to Hell. Either in this life or the next.

D eputy Wilson stood with one boot propped against the weathered pigpen, the brim of his campaign hat angled against a rare November sun. He watched the hogman toss another bucket of slop in the vicinity of his enormous pigs, and a slurry of beige mash splattered across the mud. Several pigs rushed over as the hogman looked on proudly. He was short, paunchy, and very ugly, but he had an endearing disposition that only improved when his pigs were at work.

"These pigs are as spoiled as any you'll find in this county," the hogman beamed. "I've been feeding them the mash leftover from this new brewery in Portland. It was a real inspiration on my part if I do say so. The brewery lets me have the mash for free as long as I pick it up, and the pigs are getting as fat and happy as any I've ever had."

"You're looking pretty fat and happy yourself," Wilson said.

The hogman patted his gut. "You are what you eat."

Wilson chuckled and stood up straight, half a foot taller than the hogman and solid in the layers of his tan uniform. He was clean-shaven, freshly-laundered, and not quite as young as he looked. His face was a good one, and his sergeant had once said that he was handsome enough to inspire trust, but not so handsome that men despised him immediately. He banged the top rail of the pen twice and turned to go.

"What? You can't stand here watching me feed my pigs all afternoon?"

"Unfortunately, I've gotta go try and talk some sense into Doug Jenkins before the end of the day."

"That dunce? Ask me, that boy's about fit for the penitentiary. How he's blood related to a man like Sheriff Jenkins is totally beyond my comprehension."

"He did grow up in California."

"That might explain it somewhat. Did you hear the newest scoop on him?"

Wilson shook his head.

"They're saying he fed booze to a fifteen-year-old girl and then had his way with her. Fifteen. Someone should hang him by his balls."

"You know the girl's name?"

"Oh. Well. I wouldn't book him on it yet. Rumor's been circulating. You'll have to ask around."

Wilson looked off to the northeast and nodded. "Mountain came out."

The hogman turned and gazed across his neighbor's frosted pasture. Above a crescendo of ridges all checkered with clearcuts loomed the shapely white cone of Mount St. Helens. As near as the hogman lived to it, the mountain seemed almost like another presence there amidst the conversation. Wilson and the hogman each gave the scene some reflection.

"Do you think it's true what they say?" the hogman asked.

"What's that?"

"That that sucker could blow itself to smithereens one day?"

"I have no idea."

"I just find it hard to believe that something that big and beautiful could actually . . . you know . . ." The hogman threw his hand open like a detonation and gave it the proper sound effect.

"Well, you'll be one of the first to find out, won't you."

The hogman's eyebrows knit themselves together in a look of consternation, but he soon smiled and gestured like he was shooing away a fly. "Aahh. Nothing's gonna happen to that mountain. I mean, it's a friggin mountain."

"Haven't you ever heard of Vesuvius?"

"Vesuvius? No, I haven't. Don't sound like English neither."

Wilson began to detail the cataclysm and death that distant volcano had wreaked on the surrounding populace when the hogman cut him off.

"That's enough history for me today. Ignorance is bliss. The pigs taught me that." He reached out and shook Wilson's hand. "Go on and grab yourself a package of bacon from the shop."

"That's alright. I'll get it when the whole pig's ready."

"Grab some bacon for the family. It ain't a bribe. It's an advance."

"Whatever you say, Gene. Have fun with your mash."

"Always do."

The road from the hogman's property was little more than a gravel track and badly marred by potholes. Wilson took it slowly. His tires creaked through ice-encrusted puddles while birds could be heard gossiping among the fir trees. At the neighbor's residence, a mismatched pair of Rottweilers came howling down the driveway and they refused to give up the chase until the police car had gone around the corner. The next home was set closer to the road and an elderly woman was in her yard tossing handfuls of seed to a flock of chickens. Her cottage was quite small, but it was well-maintained and behind it ran a creek. Beyond that stood timberland. When the woman noticed him coming she smiled and waved. Wilson slowed to a stop.

"How are you, Marcy?"

"I'm fine."

"How's George?"

"He's fine."

"Tell him I say hello."

"I surely will."

He tipped his hat and rolled on. At the paved intersection, his Plymouth Fury went through the corner like a sailboat and picked up speed. Ahead were several miles of cleared valley floor populated by a smattering of farmers and ranchers, but mostly by those who would prefer to be one or the other if only it were still feasible. Posted to gates and fence rails were hand-painted signs advertising fresh eggs, raw milk, puppies for sale. Another that exulted in the marvel of Jesus. The locals called the area the Chelatchie Prairie and few outside Clark County had a clue it existed at all as it was so isolated and far out in the country.

Wilson drove straight on into the setting sun as the clouds began to color up like huckleberry jam and salmon flesh. The flaring sundown was all but ethereal, and the loveliness of the land seemed especially sweet when he recalled how he had once been banished to this boondocks district. Three years later, there were folks he would take a bullet for if it meant their protection.

The streetlights were just flickering on when he entered Yacolt, a little woebegone town that had already been stagnant for fifty years and that was now teetering on the brink of collapse since the recent closure of the local lumber and plywood mill. Indian lore had it that Yacolt meant valley of the demons and there were several versions of the etymology, none of them charming. Residents pronounced the name like a smoker's cough. Wilson passed through town and parked out front Doug's Tavern across the street from the end of the railroad line.

The tavern was housed in a stout brick building that dominated the block. It had survived several forest fires that burned through the area and scourged the town in the old days. Lately, Wilson had been called here with great regularity. He reached up and unpinned the logbook from his visor, flipped through to the day's date, and jotted down the time and location, along with a few brief lines describing the nature of his visit. Then he replaced the logbook and eased himself out of the car.

His entrance aroused no special attention. Some Forest Service workers were eating burgers at one of the tall dining tables, and as he paced along the mirrored bar, he noticed an old bleary-eyed codger watching him pass with dumb wonder. A television played the nightly news above the far corner of the bar and a few men were huddled underneath it paying the screen close scrutiny. The bartender noticed Wilson coming and he said something to the others. They turned with a look of amusement. One said his name.

The bartender angled his thumb at the TV. "We're taking bets. I've got four to one these hostages don't make it out of Iran alive."

"I thought it was five to one," said another.

"That's right. Five to one. This Ayatollah dude is one bad mofo."

"And Carter's a bitch."

The bartender wore a flowery Hawaiian shirt that proclaimed *Life's a Beach* and his hair stood up in rigid, little gel spikes like rows of shark teeth. He reached back and took a bottle of Budweiser from the cooler and slid it across the bar.

Wilson merely looked at it. "What are you doing?"

"You're off duty, aren't you?"

"I'm off at six."

"I won't tell."

Wilson appeared bored.

"Okay, twist my arm," the bartender said. He lifted the bottle and drank it down halfway. A belch erupted and he began giggling like an obnoxious school boy. Wilson waited for him to quit.

"Doug, I need to chat with you a minute."

"Fire away, hombre."

"Let's grab a table."

"Ahh, these guys don't mind."

"Doug."

"Sure. Sure. Take the corner table. I'll be right over."

Wilson went and pulled out a chair. He folded one leg over the other and set his hat on the table. In a minute, Doug came over in his cartoonishly animated way. He fell into his chair like he expected it to be a foot taller.

"Whoops."

"Are you drunk?" Wilson asked.

"Is that why you're here?"

"No."

"Well, that's good. Cause, yes. I am a little drunk."

"I thought we talked about this."

"We talk about a lot of things."

Wilson exhaled and fixed him an impatient glare.

"Alright, alright. I'll switch to coffee for the rest of the shift. Okay? Honest. Now I know you didn't come in here just to bust my balls about a few drinks. What's the matter?"

"Few of the gals said you were awful rough with Elmer the other night. Said you and your buddies were kicking him around the curb for no good reason. I came to get your side of the story."

"No good reason? Terry Dingenthal caught that nut perving on his wife. First Elmer was trying to look up his old lady's skirt, then he started talking dirty to her. And it was some really raunchy stuff too. I won't even repeat it for you. Rough with Elmer? Served him right."

"You guys left some of his teeth on the sidewalk."

Doug's eyes widened and he came up in the chair. "I'm glad to hear it. Maybe it'll help keep him away from Pops and Nana."

"What's this got to do with them?"

"A creep like that living right down the street from them. I don't like it. Pops said he caught Elmer stealing from them one night. He tell you about that? I think the guy might be dangerous. And if he tries to come back in my bar again we'll kick his ass just like we did the other night. We might even burn his trailer down. Then maybe he'll go away and leave us all in peace."

Wilson glanced toward the bar and a dozen patrons threw their gazes back at their drinks. "Look, I get what you're saying, but you can't go around cracking skulls just because you feel like it. We're not on the vigilante system out here. That's what you've got me for."

"Then it's on you if that lunatic does something to Pops and Nana."

"Your Pops can still look after them both."

"Can I get back to work now?"

"Last thing. Tell me why people are talking about you and a girl too young for you to be hanging around with?"

Doug scoffed. "Unbelievable. Is this how you operate now? On the rumor mill?"

"All I asked is why I'm hearing the talk."

"People like to tell stories. I get a little bit of action here and there and all of a sudden I'm a child molester."

"So this is a jealousy thing?"

Doug raised up clumsily, his chair scraping along the floor with an awful sound.

Wilson stood swiftly and held him at bay with his palm. He leaned in closely to be sure that no one else could hear.

"It really isn't any of my business, but maybe you oughta wait until the divorce is final before you start messing around. This town's pretty small."

"Fuck off, Tom." Doug attempted to brush past, but Wilson reached out, snatched a fistful of his shirt, and drew him near once again. Doug's eyes skipped around nervously.

"You better sober up," Wilson said. "And you certainly better hope those are only rumors I've been hearing about the girl. Now, I think you've got some customers to attend to."

Wilson released his grip and Doug stumbled backwards into a stool. He took a moment to smooth out his shirt and then he turned and made his way back behind the bar.

"Well, hell. What did I miss, fellas?" Doug bantered immediately. "Any of these hostages bust loose yet? I don't see why they don't all just fly away on magic carpets."

The tension broken, there was a loud chorus of guffaws and fresh jokes about genies and wishes. Wilson put on his hat and strode to the door. The old codger waved Wilson a good night, but otherwise the barflies were relieved to see the back of him.

I t was full dark when Wilson arrived at a grand, whitewashed farmhouse sitting amidst fifty acres of prime grazing land. As he approached the residence, a donkey began braying from the corral out back, and it kept on like some exasperated bronchitic as Wilson stepped up on the front porch and knocked twice. The door opened almost immediately and a limber woman in her early seventies smiled radiantly.

"Tom," she chirped.

"How are you, Louanne?"

"I'm very well. Come on in. He's waiting for you in the den."

Wilson started to wipe his feet on the doormat, but she took him by the arm.

"Oh, don't you fuss with that. I need to sweep up anyhow."

She led him inside and closed the door and took his jacket all with a seamless elegance. Together they went down the hall discussing the weather. With her it seemed like a very fascinating subject.

They were passing along the kitchen when Wilson stopped and closed his eyes. He took in a deep breath.

"Apple pie?" He opened his eyes and found her looking slightly devious.

"Cinnamon pear," she said.

"How can you make something smell so good?"

"With love. I'll bring you a plate."

They took two steps down into a large, sweltering room that was indeed a den. The ceiling was all wooden beams sloped to the rear of the house where a woodstove crackled and hissed. Above this hung the mount of an impressive six-point elk looking incredibly virile this side of a bullet through its heart. Bookshelves brimmed, and there was a modest oak wet bar. Throughout the room hung framed law enforcement memorabilia and treasured photos from decades of service, a somewhat disordered album of Sheriff Jenkins' career from inauguration to retirement. In the corner was the old man himself, hunched over a desk and writing feverishly with a number two pencil.

Wilson started forward but Louanne stopped him and motioned that she should be the one to do it. She crept toward him saying his name with increasing volume.

"Les . . . Les . . . Lesley . . ."

Finally, she ran her fingers through his polar white hair and he flinched tremendously, banging his knee on the underside of his desk. Yowling in pain, he swiveled around and finally caught sight of Wilson.

"Tommy, my boy!" he hollered. He tried to stand and only succeeded in knocking his other knee. "Damn this desk."

"Please don't curse, dear."

"I said darn it. Now let me out of here."

"I've told you, you need one of those roller chairs."

"I wouldn't get any work done in one of those. I just need up out of here." He finally turned loose of the desk and stood with some relief, a tall man growing lean and elfin with age. "Good heavens, I must be getting old. Battling with the home furnishings. Well. Will you have a drink with me, Tommy?"

"Just one."

"Scotch?"

"Only if it's cheap. You know I can't tell them apart."

"Ah. Still an amateur, I see."

The sheriff reached into the wet bar and removed two glasses he'd had chilling. He lifted a bottle of twelve year and poured until the glasses were half full and passed one to Wilson. They raised their glasses to each other and took a sip. Wilson swallowed and examined the glass. He took another sip.

"Oh, this one's tasty."

"You're showing educability, my boy."

Louanne announced that she was about to cut the pie and asked Wilson if he'd like his à la mode. Wilson tried to protest about a spoiled appetite but the sheriff waved him off.

"Ellen can just cuss me out if she wants."

Louanne went on into the kitchen, and the sheriff gestured to the leather sofa. They took a moment to settle in.

"How's the writing going?" Wilson asked.

"Fair to middling."

"Seemed like you were on a roll just now."

The sheriff shrugged. "It's hard for me to believe anyone's going to want to read a memoir about an old hick sheriff like me. But I keep writing the thing nonetheless. Might even finish before I die."

"Will you let me read a sample?"

"Not a chance."

Wilson smiled and took another sip of his scotch. "I saw your grandson this afternoon."

The sheriff prepared himself for bad news.

"He seems worried about Elmer."

"Elmer?"

"Seems to think that Elmer might be a threat to you and Louanne. Apparently, he and a couple guys at the bar busted old Elmer up pretty good the other night."

"He didn't call you?"

"I was off, but no. He didn't call Henry either."

The sheriff clucked his tongue. "It's my fault. I shouldn't have mentioned anything to Douglas. I know how he gets."

"Why didn't you tell me?"

"Because it was nothing to worry over. Here's what happened. I was coming back from the shed the other night when I saw Elmer poking around over by the greenhouse. So I call out his name and Elmer takes off running for home. As he was scampering off I noticed that he'd dropped something so I went over and checked it out. Guess what he'd dropped?"

"A bottle of Glenfiddich."

"He'd dropped an armload of squash he'd raided from the greenhouse. Poor guy is starving over there in that trailer, I think. Nutrient deficient at the least. Louanne and I put together a basket of things and dropped it on his porch the next morning. Anonymous of course, but I'm sure he figured out where it came from. I'd like him to know that he can just ask for something if he's hungry. God knows we've got plenty."

"You sure you aren't worried about him?"

"Elmer? Nah. He gets a little wacky without his meds, but I don't see a violent streak in him. Just a sad sack is all."

"Well, I want you to keep me informed."

"Of course." He clapped his hands. "Hey now, what's going on? Where's the dang pie we've been promised? Louanne?"

"Yes dear?" she called with mock annoyance.

"I thought me and this fine deputy had some pie coming to us."

"Oh, shoot."

There was a bustle of noises from the kitchen and in a minute she reappeared with two plates. She handed them off and was heading back to the kitchen when the sheriff called her name again. She spun around with a retort half formed.

"Are we supposed to eat this with our fingers?"

"Oh, my goodness."

Right then the phone in the kitchen started ringing and Louanne went and picked it up. The sheriff set his plate on the coffee table and Wilson did the same.

"Telemarketer," the sheriff said. "She'll just be a minute."

Wilson signaled that it was no matter.

"So? We still going hunting this weekend?" the sheriff asked.

"We'd better be. Otherwise I'm cleaning gutters."

"That's my boy. Can you be here by six?"

"Sure. You want me to drive?"

"I drive. I may be retired, but I still outrank you. Besides that, I know all the roads you only think you know."

Wilson smiled. "You been scouting much this year?"

"Some. Saw a pretty good herd up around Yale the other day. Snow seems to have finally driven them down into the valleys."

"Think McAllister will let us pop one on his property?"

"Hell, no. I already begged him. The man seems to think those elk are his personal pets. He's got his wife and kids out there practically feeding them by hand. One of those McAllisters is bound to get gored."

"Well, I suppose I'd rather hunt up by the mountain anyhow."

The sheriff slapped at his knee. "I keep forgetting to tell you. I saw them a couple weeks ago clear up on the summit of Mount St Helens."

"The McAllisters?"

"Elk. A whole herd of elk."

"On the summit?"

"Yes."

Wilson was squinting with disbelief.

"Heck, it was in the paper."

The sheriff lifted out of his seat and went rummaging through a stack of newspapers saved up for fire starter. Wilson glanced at the plates, the ice cream already going soupy from the heat of the pie. He looked to see if Louanne was still on the phone, but she was out of sight and the receiver hung back in place. The sheriff returned with the paper and withdrew a pair of spectacles from his shirt pocket.

"And I quote . . . *Bands of elk apparently terrified by hunters' gunfire climbed to the summit of Mount St. Helens over the weekend but had returned to lower elevations by this morning. Longtime residents of the area . . . that would be me . . . and wildlife agents say this is the first time they have ever heard of elk on the summit of the nine thousand five hundred foot mountain.*"

"Are they interbreeding with mountain goats or what?"

"Just some desperate elk, I think. Apparently, a couple of them got so scared up there they plummeted to their death."

"Bad way to go."

"Yeah, but getting shot in the ass isn't any better."

The sheriff tossed the paper absently to the coffee table and noticed the ice cream pooling up on the plates. He looked for Louanne, scratched his head, and winced.

"This kind of situation right here is starting to scare me."

"What do you mean?"

The sheriff gave him a look signifying that now was not the time and then picked up the plates. He beckoned for Wilson to follow and they went into the kitchen. Louanne was standing at the counter flipping through a booklet of coupons with a mouthful of pie and her fork going for another. She caught them in her peripheral and looked up with a smile that quickly went sour when she saw their plates.

She swallowed. "Oh, my dear heavens."

Even with his eyes closed Wilson would have known he was approaching Longview. Most days the sulfuric funk of the pulp and paper mills was as foul as though he'd messed himself. Sad as it was, it smelled like home.

He entered the city as a long, graffitied train clacked along the lumber yards and log ponds and landfill. Beyond this the mills glowed with innumerable orange lights like some sleepless festival while plumes of chemicals billowed from the smokestacks toward a bright, bronze moon. It was the only home he'd ever known, and God willing, he hoped to keep it that way until the day he died.

His neighborhood was a stone's throw from Lake Sacajawea and overhung with gigantic oak trees whose limbs made a latticework of shadows on the cobbled streets. Most of the homes were big two-story American dreams, but Wilson and his wife tended toward frugality. Theirs was perhaps the smallest house on the block, a modest but attractive Craftsman that hunkered behind a carefully tended garden. The lights were on in the kitchen, and Wilson watched his wife's silhouette shifting in the curtains as he parked and gathered his things.

He was hanging his hat and jacket in the hall closet as Duke came around the corner with his tail wagging.

"Hey there, pup."

The lanky, half-grown German shepherd trotted over, sniffing audibly. Wilson went to pet him and Duke leapt to snatch at the bacon. He waved the package away like a matador and the dog landed with a look of recalculation.

"Ellen, your mutt is a nuisance," he called.

"He's a purebred," she hollered back from the kitchen.

"You'll get none of this," Wilson told the dog, which had backed up and was sitting on his haunches.

In a small safe hidden deep in the closet Wilson deposited his gun and badge and cuffs. He kicked off his shoes and scooted them inside and then took a bone-shaped treat from the shelf. Wilson displayed the treat to Duke who was trembling with anticipation when suddenly the dog yelped and flew sideways against the wall.

"Daddy!" his little girl screamed, thrashing her way toward him and barreling straight into his chest.

"Maggie, you can't be so rough with the dog," he said as he tossed the treat to the floor.

"I missed you, Daddy."

"Yes, I missed you too. But did you hear me? You need to be nice to Duke."

"Okay."

"Okay. Say, sorry, Duke."

"I'm sorry, Duke, for hitting you into the wall."

"There. That's nice."

Duke was cracking the treat into pieces and eating them one at a time as Wilson lifted his daughter up like a doll. She wrapped her arms around his neck and they went on into the kitchen where Ellen was sautéing vegetables. She was a marvelously wholesome looking blonde and just beginning to show her pregnancy beneath her apron. She blew some stray hair from her eyes and turned from the stove.

"It's awfully hard to cook for a man who comes home whenever he feels like."

"You're really gonna be irritated with me then. They wouldn't let me leave unless I ate a slice of Louanne's pie. À la mode. Well, sort of."

She rolled her eyes. "You'd better get over here and kiss me then so I forget all about it."

He shifted his daughter to the other arm and walked over and rested his hand on Ellen's belly.

"How's our little peanut?"

"Very happy."

"And how's mama?"

"Hungry."

They kissed warmly, and as they did the little girl's eyes skipped from one to the other with delight.

"I need a kiss too," Maggie announced.

"You do, huh." Wilson kissed her on the cheek with an exaggerated smack and set her down on the hardwood floor.

"What do you have there?" Ellen asked.

"Gene sent me home with some bacon."

At this Maggie began shouting *bacon, bacon* while pacing around in circles and pumping her arm erratically like a marching band leader gone utterly berserk.

Wilson chuckled. "You know, that's about how I feel too."

Their supper was a simple and hearty roast and they lingered over it as Wilson sipped from a glass of cheap red wine. Country music played quietly from the radio.

Wilson folded up his napkin and laid it on his plate. "So, Lesley's pretty worried about Louanne."

"What for?" Ellen asked.

"I think he thinks she might be starting to lose her marbles."

"That's not a nice way of putting it."

"Well, put it however you want."

"What does he think is going on with her?"

"I don't know, but it was a little strange how forgetful she was tonight."

"There's plenty of explanations for that. Especially with everything they've got going on out there."

"I suppose. But then it seems like he would know best." He took a drink of wine. "Let's just not ever get old."

Her eyes shot at him and her breath seemed to catch, her expression looking both frightened and ferocious. "Don't you ever talk like that."

"What—"

"Don't you ever say something like you're not going to grow old with me."

"What's gotten into you?"

She was on the verge of tears as she reached back and took the daily paper from the counter and set it on the table before him. The lead story told of a Portland policeman who'd been shot in the head while serving a drug warrant. Wilson had already heard all about it at the station. He gave the paper a brief scan and then waited patiently for her to continue.

"You better keep on coming home," she said. "You hear me? Don't you let nothing or nobody take you away from me."

"I thought you had gotten over that."

"I thought I had too, but I haven't. I can't. It's alright. You just keep coming home."

I t had been raining all day and it was raining still. Wilson cruised through the weeping country as his windshield wipers kept a ragged beat, the sky like a sad old mattress that seemed to sag atop the trees. A long file of vehicles approached behind the lead of a school bus and they whooshed by like the cars of a train, their tires slishing up ephemeral tracks in the pavement. The hobby farms and small ranches all looked bleary and dismal and Wilson liked to see the horses standing out in the mud, dignified despite the weather.

At the outskirts of Amboy, Wilson turned into a puddly gravel lot and parked. He was walking up to the warehouse he'd been called to when a rusted little Chevette came screaming around the corner, a frail white car with loose belts whirring like a swarm of cicadas. Its rear end fishtailed, and a passing car was forced to veer outside its lane. The driver may or may not have seen Wilson and the car quickly picked up speed, leaving behind an acrid aftersmell of neglect. Wilson was shaking his head.

"Goddamnit, Rodney. Slow the fuck down."

He turned and walked up to the warehouse, a dingy, little shack of a thing. He knocked the metal door clanging twice and stepped inside. There was the immediate aroma of cedar and moss and fir branches. Raindrops plinked on the metal roof. A few low-wattage light bulbs hung from the rafters, and as Wilson's eyes adjusted to the poorly lit room he noticed three women sitting around a wooden table. One of them stood to receive him.

"Officer, I think we figured out who did it." She had a severe set of eyebrows and hair like she'd been licking batteries.

"That would sure be nice," Wilson said. "But first why don't you tell me your names."

"I'm Peggy. That's Lucy. And she's Marge."

Wilson wrote the names in his notepad and then surveyed the room with interest. Everywhere lay heaps of ferns and reeds and funguses and pine cones and dried hornets' nests and many other botanical forms that Wilson could not identify. On the table there were gardening clippers, packing tape and order forms. Near the door stood a stack of boxes of various sizes. Wilson readied his pen.

"And this is a . . . Well now, what is this place exactly?"

"We're a flower shop supplier. Wholesale delivery. We already discussed all this with the dispatcher. Look, we know who did it."

"Alright, Peggy. Just hang on. So how did the suspect enter your warehouse?"

"Just walked right on in."

"Was there forcible entry?"

"They certainly had no right to be in here."

"Yes, but how did they gain access to the warehouse? Did they punch through a window or break the lock on the door?"

"Wasn't any lock on the door."

"I see."

"Never figured there was anything in here that anybody'd think worth stealing. Always thought this was a pretty trustworthy neighborhood."

"And what all did you find missing?"

"I already told the dispatcher. They took all three of our shovels."

"Shovels. And what else went missing?"

DEEP FIRE RISE

"Just the shovels. And we're none too happy about it either cause they was some real nice shovels."

"They didn't mess with anything else? Nothing out of the fridge over there? They didn't bother with the radio or saws or any of your ferns?"

"Like I said already, they only took the shovels and that's how come we know who it is."

Lucy and Marge had been following the interview like a pair of cautious ewes. They wore heavy sweatshirts against the cold and they looked in need of a shower. Wilson smiled at them and they smiled back uncertainly. He turned to Peggy.

"So you think you can identify the thief."

"That's what I've been saying. We think it must be the undertakers."

Wilson paused in his notetaking. He took a moment.

"You believe multiple grave diggers stole your shovels? Do you have any other evidence for me to go on?"

"In this economy? Shoot. A good shovel ain't cheap. Besides that, the graveyard is just around the corner and I don't get along with them at all. They've been burying agnostics if you can even believe that."

He was working out how to extricate himself from the shack when there was a knock on the door. A man poked his face in.

"Okay for me to come in?" he called.

"It's okay, Dwayne," Peggy replied.

A pudgy bald man stepped inside shaking himself of the rain.

"What did you need?" she asked.

The man was just noticing Wilson and a clouded look came over his face. "Say, he's not here on account of those shovels, is he?"

Wilson flipped his notepad shut.

"Shoot. I got 'em out in the truck. Never thought you would've even noticed 'em missing."

All afternoon it kept on drizzling. The dreariness of the weather was something Wilson had long ago stopped resisting. He made a languid lap of his district, taking turns at random, his eyes attuned to disorder and finding none more than the usual. The dispatcher had nothing for anybody, crime generally favoring fair weather. The hours stretched long and they were filled with the opinions of men on the radio.

Later in the day, at an hour as gray as the last, he turned up a dead-end forest road where he sometimes jumped deer. The road was lined with jack firs the size of Christmas trees, and he was rousing chickadees and nuthatches all along the way. At the end of the road there were two trucks parked one behind the other. There was no sign of either driver.

Wilson stopped thirty yards back and tried to reach the dispatcher to run the plates. There was no response and he tried again and then hung up the mic for his radio was out of range. He took down his logbook and was recording the license plates when a man's head and bare shoulders popped up in the rear window of the front truck. The man spotted the squad car and disappeared. Wilson chuckled to himself and shifted to park.

A minute later the driver's door was kicked open, followed by a pair of boots and then the rest of the man. He was an awfully good-looking fellow with bulging arms and a toothsome smile.

Wilson stepped out to meet him.

"I did not see you there," the man said with a thick Russian accent. "Something I did wrong?"

"Not necessarily. I'm just on patrol."

"Okay. I see. And this is part of your patrol? This little road?"

"I try to patrol all the roads in my district."

The man was nodding and smiling vigorously. "This is very good. Keeping us safe, yes?"

Wilson was looking at the vehicles. A woman, young and blond, sat upright and fixed her hair. The man had his thumbs in his pockets and he rocked up onto his toes. Wilson saw how hard he was trying to look relaxed.

"Is she eighteen?" he asked.

"She says that she is twenty."

"Then take her on home where you ought to be and have a nice day." Wilson was already heading back to his car.

"Thank you, sir. I mean, officer."

He slid into his seat and took down the logbook, recording the second license plate number below the first. Alongside them Wilson wrote some filthy cop jargon and then he tossed the logbook to the passenger seat and backed down the road.

His standard twelve-hour shift crawled along listlessly. He whiled away an hour or more at the Fargher Lake General Store sipping coffee and listening to the collective gossip that was like a form a currency among the locals. Wilson waited for an old-timer to finish a story about a vicious rooster his neighbor kept letting loose and then he refilled his coffee and walked outside. A man called out his name. Wilson stepped back under the dripping eaves as a mechanic in greasy blue overalls approached bearing his hand.

"How you holding up?" the mechanic asked as they shook.

"Still alive, so I guess I can't complain."

"Woke up on the top side of dirt again, eh."

"I try to keep it a habit."

They watched a postal service van turn off the highway and pull up to the curb, the rain showing slantwise in the beams of its headlights. The mailman left the van running and he walked up wiping the wetness from his bald head.

"I wouldn't want to be you today," the mechanic said.

"I don't want to be me either."

"Ever heard of a hat?"

"I lost it to a Doberman."

"Really?"

"Yes."

Without further elaboration, the mailman walked inside the store. Wilson and the mechanic looked at each other.

"Bad day for him," the mechanic said with a wheezy chuckle that morphed right into a lingering cough. His lungs finally caught hold of something, and he hawked a wad of phlegm out onto the asphalt.

"There's something I've been meaning to talk to you about," the mechanic continued. "Any way you could go talk to the Vertner kid for me?"

"Rodney?"

"Yeah. That boy's been tearing around these roads like he's got a death wish. He damn near ran over our dog, and he did sideswipe the Michaelson's fence. Only reason it didn't come down is cause the old man knows how to dig a decent post hole. I know all about the Vertner family's trouble, but something's gotta be done about that kid. If he keeps on the way he's going he's gonna wind up killing himself or a neighbor or both."

"I hear ya. Do me a favor and call these things in to dispatch."

"Well. That's not really my style. Out here I think solutions ought to be a bit more personable. Just promise me you'll talk to him."

"I might be able to get over there before dark."

"You're a fine man."

Wilson cruised back toward town. He wondered if he was making a mistake getting involved so near the end of his day but he went nonetheless. He half hoped he'd find someone worth pulling over along the way but all the passing cars were properly registered and running at or under the speed limit. It was still raining as he entered Yacolt.

The house was near the center of town, a dilapidated abode that stood out even in that hapless neighborhood. The roof was mostly disintegrated and covered with tarps, and the siding was at least three different shades of gloom. The front lawn seemed like some graveyard for children's toys while half of the driveway was occupied by an old Ford pickup that had been resting on blocks for months. Parked along the curb was the rusted white Chevette he'd seen earlier and on the other half of the driveway stood Virgil Vertner, a wiry middle-aged man wearing glasses and suspenders and just heaving into a powerful axe swing. He was chopping his way through a full cord of wood and his axehead came down with a resounding thwack as the wood split and the pieces tumbled amongst the growing pile. He was reaching for another piece when he noticed Wilson. He swung the axe into the chopping block and limped over to the squad car. Wilson rolled his window down.

"I thought you said you were done chopping in the rain?"

"I'd rather eat than be good to my word." Virgil removed his glasses and wiped them on his shirt. "It's the arthritis that's really ruining my day."

"I've never seen you hobbling quite that bad."

Virgil replaced his glasses, but they started beading up again almost immediately. "Days like today I figure I must have done some real devilish things in my former life. At least I hope I did. Otherwise this whole thing ain't even close to fair."

Wilson was remembering the call, the scene in the backyard, the look on his dead wife's face. Virgil saw in Wilson everything he was seeing.

"Now don't you start going there," Virgil said. "Don't you even do it."

"I'm sorry, Virgil."

"And don't you be sorry neither. Sorriness ain't worth shit. Now what'd you need me for?"

Right then the screen door banged shut, and Virgil's son came walking down the porch. Wilson nodded toward him and Virgil swiveled in his direction and hollered.

"Damnit, Rodney. What in the hell did you do this time?"

"I didn't do anything," came the petulant reply.

The boy was still in high school and he wore a frayed black sweatshirt and a pathetic little mustache that made him look oddly Mexican. He had a bouncy gait, but there was a menacing blankness to his eyes. He stood there beside his father.

"Well, what'd he do?" Virgil asked.

"I just need him to start driving with more care."

The boy was already beginning to snivel out some sort of rebuttal when Virgil squeezed the back of his neck. The boy reared back like an unbroken horse but he quieted down. Wilson continued.

"Chill out, Rodney. I'm not here to get you in trouble."

"Well, it seems like you are."

"Well, I'm not. I'm just telling you that you need to take it easy. I saw you fishtailing around the corner out by Amboy and until we get your tabs in order you're not even supposed to be driving at all."

"You're just here cause somebody's been complaining about me again."

"I'm here because I saw you driving like a maniac with my own eyes."

"Everybody's always pitching crap on me."

"Cool down, Rodney."

"I'm always the no good fuck up. Well, fuck that!"

"Hold on now."

The boy came totally unleashed and the rage in him was astounding. His whole body flexed and his fists balled and he went looking for the proper thing to pummel. When he came to the chain-link gate he gave it a fierce one two and busted the latch. Already his right hand was bleeding and before he made it back up the porch steps he spun around and made a gun with his thumb and forefinger and pointed it at his temple.

"Maybe I oughta just kill myself and be done with it!" he screamed.

He swung open the front door and slammed it shut and the screen banged after.

"What's going on with him?" Wilson asked.

"Oh, he just thinks everybody in town is picking on him."

"Well, the way he's been driving they've got a right to."

"I know that."

"And he needs to get those tabs taken care of."

"I know it. It's just that money's been real tight ever since the mill closed."

"I already told Rodney I'd pay the fee. All he needs to do is come down to the office with me and we'll get it taken care of."

"I know that and I appreciate you helping take him under your wing."

"Just tell me a day that'll work and we'll go make it happen. But it's gotta get done."

The screen door swung open again and they watched the boy stride toward the center of town.

"He's just gotta blow off some steam is all," Virgil said.

"Why don't you have him help you chop that wood?"

"Would you trust him with an axe?"

They both laughed.

"You need some firewood?" Virgil asked.

"I've already got too much. But I'll keep an ear to the ground for you."

"I'll chop anything right now. It's the only thing that's keeping us afloat."

"I'll let you know."

The day was through and the sky had started to darken to dusk. Wilson still had some paperwork to finish at the station so he began heading west. He'd only driven the first few miles when the dispatcher called for him.

A young man was reported pointing a gun at cars in the street. He was last seen heading west on Yacolt and Railroad. The suspect was wearing jeans and a black sweatshirt. Dark hair. Approximately five feet nine inches and a hundred and forty pounds.

Wilson jerked on the wheel and his tires squealed as he doubled back toward town. He picked up the radio mic. "Ten four and en route."

He'd nearly made it back into Yacolt when the radio sounded again.

An attendant at the Trading Post just reported that our suspect entered the store and pointed a gun at her and then ran away. Caution is advised.

Wilson copied the dispatch and hung up the mic.

"Rodney doesn't have a gun," he said to himself. He thought about it for a moment. "I really hope Rodney doesn't have a gun."

Wilson entered town. He searched all the most likely streets in the vicinity but there was no sign of Rodney. He pulled up to the Trading Post and the female attendant was standing in the doorway waving to flag him down. Wilson parked and hurried under the storefront awning. The attendant was plump and pimpled and her demeanor was of someone accustomed to such situations.

"Young guy came in here soaking wet and asking for a pack of cigarettes," she began. "I asked to see his ID, and all of a sudden he pulled out a gun and pointed it at me."

"Are you sure it was a gun?"

"It definitely looked like a gun."

"But are you sure?"

She stared off into her memory and back again. "I suppose I couldn't swear to it. But it was definitely metal. It was shiny like that."

"Do you know the guy?"

"I don't know his name, but I've seen him around. Young guy. Black sweatshirt. Sort of looks like a Mexican."

"Did he say anything when he had the object pointed at you?"

"No. He just raised it up at me for a second and then ran away."

"Did he take the cigarettes?"

"Nope. Just left 'em. The whole thing was fast. The kid seemed . . . I don't know. He seemed twisted. Like he was on drugs maybe. Or maybe just unhinged. I don't know. His eyes were really frightening."

Wilson thanked her for her time and promised to follow up. Back in his car he updated the dispatcher and then drove on to the Vertner place. Virgil was still chopping wood by a single spotlight plugged into the garage. When he noticed Wilson, he rested his axe on his shoulder and waited.

"Did Rodney make it back home yet?" Wilson asked.

"He ran on in the house just a minute ago."

"Is he in for the night now?"

"He's in. He's just cooling off in his room. He'll stay in."

"Virgil. Rodney doesn't have a gun, does he?"

"A gun? No."

"Are you absolutely certain about that?"

"Don't have no guns around anymore. Don't know where he would have gotten one."

"Rodney's going to be in a lot of trouble if it turns out otherwise."

"What's it this time?"

"Some folks are saying he was pointing a gun at them . . ."

Virgil took a long, pained breath and let it out sadly.

". . . But my guess is that it was a wrench or a piece of pipe or something."

"Just don't see where he would've gotten a gun."

"Make sure he stays in tonight, will ya?"

"I'll chain him down if I have to."

As Wilson drove off he could see Virgil in the rearview mirror, the gimpy woodworker standing there motionless with a pitiable look on his face as he absorbed the brunt of yet another downturn. Wilson was just turning the corner when Virgil hefted his axe again. He still had to load the entire cord of wood that night.

Wilson's desk was small and tidy and his cubicle only nominally partitioned from the rest of the sheriff's office. On his pinboard he'd tacked pictures of his wife, his daughter, and him and his father holding up a pair of Chinook salmon. His calendar was more a schedule of games for the Portland Trail Blazers, and his one frame contained the faded sepia image of a childhood dog. He was nearly finished with his report when a uniformed giant stood against his faux wall. His voice was like Zeus personified.

"You about done with that?" the giant asked.

"What's up?"

"You gotta hear Troy's story before he leaves."

"Give me three minutes."

The giant went and fixed himself a cup of coffee and stood stirring it with a miniature straw. He was at least six and a half feet tall and his boots were enormous.

In the center of the room was a heavy plastic table littered with various pamphlets and newspapers and pictures of suspected criminals to watch

JON GOSCH

for. At the far end of the table sat a serious looking deputy with a buzzcut and an immaculate uniform. He was cleaning his pistol with great care and his ear perked up every time there was something on the police scanner.

Wilson finally set down his pen, stapled his papers together, and went and stood next to the giant who seemed giddy as a kindergartner.

"Tell him the story, Troy."

Troy set his gun down and commenced in a deadpan droll. "Got called to a restaurant about ten thirty last night. A drunk and disorderly. Get there and this girl's been throwing plates around . . ."

"Was she trying to start a food fight or something?" Wilson asked.

"She was just being a childish bitch as far as I could tell. Even her friends wanted her out of there. So I tell her it's time to go and start leading her out and the whole time she's giving me a ration of shit. I get her outside and I'm about to put the cuffs on her, you know, just to humiliate her, when she spins around and spits a loogie right into my eyes."

"Bad move."

"Didn't like that at all, so I reached back and slapped her across the face."

Wilson shook his head and looked around the room to see who else might be listening.

"Once I'd scrounged her out of the hedge she'd tumbled into, I put the cuffs on her extra tight and threw her in the back of my car. We'd just started booking her for the drunk and disorderly when her dad shows up at the station. We start telling him about what she'd been up to at the restaurant when the girl starts blubbering about, he hit me, daddy. He slapped me, and on and on."

The giant nudged Wilson with his elbow. "This is the best part."

"The dad looks at me and says, did you slap my daughter, and I say, yes. He says, why did you slap my daughter, and I say, because she spit in my face, sir. The guy turns to his daughter and says, did you spit in this officer's face? She says, yep, I did, and the guy rears up and smacks her off the stool she was sitting on."

The giant had fallen into Wilson, his shoulders heaving as he thundered out guffaws. "Isn't that the greatest story you've ever heard?"

Troy finally cracked a smile. "Afterwards her dad told me I was the finest cop he'd ever met."

"No shit," Wilson said.

"No shit."

"How did it feel to slap the girl?"

"How did it feel?" Troy cocked his head philosophically and then shrugged. "Can't really say how it felt. Just something that needed to be done."

The giant was pointing at Troy and shaking his head toward Wilson. "He's cold-blooded as a croc."

"You guys hear about the detective from Gresham?" Wilson asked.

Troy leaned back and clarified, "You mean the former detective from Gresham?"

"I didn't hear about this," said the giant.

"Dumbass stole a hundred and thirty-eight pounds of marijuana from the evidence room," Wilson said. "Already pled guilty to first degree theft and delivery of a controlled substance."

"Not very smooth for a detective."

"Thought he could get away with substituting the pot with a bale of alfalfa."

"Yeah, cause those look real similar," said Troy.

"So how'd they pin it on him?" asked the giant.

"Not sure exactly, but somebody with the Multnomah Sheriff's Department noticed the switch and triggered the investigation."

"Shit," said Troy. "The Multnomah cops were just pissed that this detective got to their stash before they did. Bunch of shaggy-haired hippies down in Oregon. You hear they were trying to legalize pot in Eugene? Won't be long before they're putting dope in school lunches."

Wilson gave the giant a pat on the back. "It's five past six, boys. I'm outta here."

"Hold on," called Troy. "What ended up happening with the Vertner kid? Don't send me out there blind."

"I got a couple reports that he was pointing a gun at people—"

"So I heard."

"But I'm about ninety-nine percent sure that he just had a wrench or a piece of pipe or something like that. His dad swears there's no guns in the house."

"Doesn't mean the kid didn't get a hold of one."

"The gal at the gas station backed off her statement. I'm telling you. Ninety-nine percent it was a piece of pipe or something."

"Maybe so, but he's still threatening people."

"What's this kid's problem?" asked the giant.

"Emotional duress," said Wilson.

"About what?"

"His mom walked out in their backyard a couple weeks ago and blew her brains out."

"Fuck me."

The police scanner started up and they listened as the dispatcher told of a peeping Tom reportedly prowling an apartment complex in Battle Ground.

"Did she leave a suicide note?" the giant asked.

"Yeah."

'What'd it say?"

"It said, I can't do this anymore."

"Who found the body?"

"Who do you think?"

S now fell soundlessly in the haven of his backyard. The fence and the fountain and the birdhouses and the lawn had all grown two inches overnight. Wilson spectated from the veranda as wisps of steam curled from his coffee cup. This was his favorite hour, this Saturday darkness when the town was still. Not even the paperboys were up yet. He watched the snow until the flakes began fluttering to a halt and then he checked his watch, finished his coffee, and went inside.

At the end of the hall he paused to watch them from the doorway, his wife and daughter and dog entwined upon the bed in a disheveled heap of blankets and fur and polka dot pajamas. He could not tell which one of them was snoring. He padded forward and kissed his daughter on the forehead and then moved to his wife and traced her hair behind her ear. She took a deep breath and stirred.

"Don't go," she murmured.

"They'd be waiting on me."

"Stay and snuggle with us."

"You've got all the company you need." He kissed her on the lips. "I'll be home for dinner."

"You better get a big one."

"We know just where they're at."

The streets of Longview were unplowed and as empty as he'd ever seen them. Under the glow of the streetlamps the snow was discolored and looked like sand. In some places Wilson was the first to travel that morning, and his truck compressed a rutted pair of trails as he crunched along in four-wheel drive. At a red light he watched a Camaro turn out of a gas station and keep on turning until it had spun around and drifted into the opposite lane. The driver progressed and slid straight to the curb. Wilson's traffic light blinked green and he drove on through town.

Out on the interstate the lanes were all covered with chunks of slush that were being passed back and forth between the cars like some anarchistic winter sport. Southbound rigs rumbled along in chains while an occasional northbound driver pulled to the shoulder to cinch theirs on. At Carrolls the highway bent along with the bank of the Columbia and Wilson looked out on that big black river as it twinkled with the reflection of the moon. Farther out in the channel a cargo ship was chugging upriver for Portland and it crossed in front of the nuclear plant cooling tower that rose up massively from the Oregon shore like the most toxic mushroom that ever grew.

There was still no sign of dawn when Wilson spotted the Jenkins' homemade mailbox. He turned and powered up their drive, passing a dozen cows huddled together amidst one of their fields and looking like they were already bored with the weather. Wilson made the corner above the pond, and he almost turned right around when he spotted the yellow Jeep parked in the driveway.

His headlights washed over the sheriff's derelict grandson who had raised an arm to shield his eyes. Wilson pulled alongside the Jeep and killed his lights and then took some time to gather his things. He was thinking he should have just stayed in bed when there came a rapping on his window.

Wilson cranked a few turns on the handle. "Good morning, Doug."

"Well, what do you think, brotha? Do I look like a hunter or what?"

Doug held his arms aloft and did a little spin, and Wilson looked him over. From head to foot Doug's attire was orange as a jack-o'-lantern.

Pants, vest and hat all bright and fiery. Doug was smiling expectantly, like a contestant in a pageant.

Wilson couldn't help but laugh. "I think if we put the high beams on you for a few minutes, your outfit would glow in the dark."

Doug seemed confused. "It's hunter orange."

"I see that."

"Pops told me if I wanted to come hunting I needed to buy some proper clothes."

"I'm sure he meant for you to get some camo. You only need hunter orange for the modern rifle season."

Doug looked at himself.

"Besides that, it's only the vest that's required."

"I spent ninety bucks on this stuff."

"Is it at least waterproof?"

"I don't know."

"Didn't you ever go hunting where you lived in California?"

"It wasn't that kind of a place."

Wilson tossed Doug a jacket and an extra pair of jeans and walked up toward the house as a rooster began to crow back by the garden. He gave the door a couple perfunctory knocks and stepped inside.

The sheriff was there in the hallway with his hands on his hips. Before Wilson could speak, he said, "I know, I know."

"Does he even know how to load a gun?"

"He's gotta start somewhere."

"You could have at least told me he was coming."

"And then you would have stayed in bed."

"Maybe."

"Look. The boy's been begging me to bring him along. What am I supposed to say? Anyways, Douglas is the least of my worries this morning."

"What's the matter?"

The sheriff pointed toward the kitchen and as if on cue there came Louanne's voice muffled by the walls.

"I swear I made those sandwiches last night. I'm sure I did. They have got to be in this fridge somewhere."

The sheriff raised his eyebrows and blew out his cheeks in a look of exasperation. Wilson took a few steps and peered around the corner. Louanne was crouched before the refrigerator shuffling jars and Tupperware containers from shelf to shelf. Wilson stepped back out of sight.

"It's okay, dear," the sheriff tried. "We'll just whip up a couple of new sandwiches."

"They're in here," she barked.

The sheriff picked up a rifle that had been leaning against the wall and passed it to Wilson. "Would you mind showing Douglas some of the basics? We'll be out of the house in a few minutes."

The road to the hunting grounds was high above the reservoir and as slick and twisty as an amusement ride. The sheriff bent his battered red Chevy truck around another hairpin turn, and Wilson looked down into a pit of complete blackness. Somewhere a thousand feet below the Lewis River was pooling up against its confines, spinning turbines unseen. Wilson trusted the sheriff, but even so he would have felt better if he were driving. The sheriff seemed barely aware of the road. He was toggling dials on the CB radio as Doug called from the backseat.

"Pops, are you sure you're watching where you're going? It's pretty steep on this side. And with the snow . . ."

The sheriff left one hand on the wheel and turned around almost fully in his seat. "You know how many times I've driven this road?"

"Just want us to stay safe is all."

The sheriff winked at Wilson and went back to the CB. He played the squelch back and forth until a voice came through clearly. *Up the valley at the one and a half,* said a log truck driver with an alacrity unusual for the hour.

Dawn was near and the sky became as murkily blue as the depths of the ocean. The sheriff turned off on a gravel road that climbed through second-growth Douglas fir of mixed ages. When they got up to the top of a bald landing he rolled down the windows and shut off the engine.

There was supreme quiet, only the wind huffing through the valley below. The four of them stayed in silence as the shapes of the forest found their contours and then their complexion in the ever-bluing light. Another day on earth arriving by tiptoe.

Everyone but Doug wore camouflaged attire from stocking cap to hiking boot and they were all armed with fifty-caliber black powder rifles loaded from the muzzle. When it was light enough to legally shoot, they stepped out past a crude fire pit and a colorful array of spent shotgun shells and stood at the edge of the landing. At that elevation a tremendous amount of land was fast becoming visible. Ridge after ridge flowed out before them like the rolling sea and fog basked in each successive vale like lakes of cotton. It had all been evergreens once, countless millions of fir and spruce and cedar carpeting every nook and crag of this rumpled terrain. Now the clearcuts were the dominant feature, entire hillsides and ridgetops scalped to the bleeding soil and an eyesore for those possessing even the meagerest of souls. Yet it was in these open places that the hunters focused their attention.

Wilson and the sheriff brought binoculars to their eyes and glassed along the timberlines. They made a serious study of the landscape, scrutinizing every possible rump or antler, letting their eyes go soft and then hard and then soft again. Louanne spotted the elk naked eyed. She tapped the sheriff on the shoulder and pointed uphill twice. Five cows were grazing nonchalantly at the edge of a small clearcut. They were perhaps seventy yards away on a slight slope. The sheriff put his thumb up and nodded.

Louanne swung her rifle from her shoulder, looking surprisingly suited to the task. The sheriff whispered, aim high. She flicked the safety forward, crouched just a tad, and took aim at of the cow most broadside.

The sound of the gunfire was enormous and lingered upon the land. Smoke rose from the rifle. The cows looked up from their forage, each of them standing erect and trying to make sense of the noise. A few of them began picking their way to the timber. The sheriff took Louanne's rifle and gave her his own. She aimed at a cow that had not yet moved and the shot rang out as she lowered the rifle. All five cows took off running. The sheriff told Wilson and Doug to fire away, but the elk were already disappearing into the timber.

The sheriff and Louanne looked at each other. She lifted her shoulders. "I don't know."

"Maybe there's some blood we can follow," Wilson said.

The four of them trudged up the hillside, weaving their way around stumps and brush piles and sticker bushes. They made it to where the cows had been feeding and scoured the terrain, but found no sign of blood.

"Couldn't have asked for a better shot," the sheriff said matter-of-factly.

Louanne shrugged again. "I just don't know."

"I've missed 'em closer than that," Wilson said. "Slope like that, there's no such thing as an easy shot."

"I think she didn't really have her heart in it," the sheriff said. "She gets sentimental sometimes with the cows."

"Will you hush already," she said.

He smiled at her with great affection. "Lots of daylight, dear. You'll get the next one."

They drove on to another clearcut where they might still find elk at their early morning feeding. The sheriff smoked and steered as Louanne told tales of their grandchildren and Doug pretended that he wasn't drowsing. Here and there Wilson pointed out where the elk had been running, their cleft hoofprints preserved in the snow and the mud of the roadbank. They crossed a tumultuous creek that rushed loudly under the road and Wilson had them stop. A stand of alders grew along the waterway and one of the biggest trees was without bark at antler level and worn down to a fine smooth varnish.

"Big old bull did that," the sheriff said.

"Looks pretty fresh," Wilson agreed.

"Come on out, you brute. Give us some meat."

As they rounded the next corner they could see down into a deep ravine where foggy vapors were broiling out the hillside like the breath of a dragon from a hidden lair. Beyond that the higher land was thick with snow, and above it the clouds were scudding away to reveal a thinner blue realm. They passed a freshly charred clearcut still smoldering and steaming from a recent slash burn, and there were stacks of Douglas firs awaiting conveyance to the mills in Longview and Camas. The road became steep and circular and the Chevy chugged for all it was worth. Finally, they ascended to a muddy promontory and there was Mount St. Helens to the north, a colossal beauty that rose up in a perfect cone to nearly ten thousand feet.

"Elk were on the summit of that?" Wilson said.

The sheriff flicked his cigarette out the window. "On the tippy top."

By midmorning the sun was shining and much of the snow was already beginning to melt. Wilson found himself walking a remote logging road with Doug in the lead. The trough along the road and the road itself trickled with thaw and they ambled on at an easy pace, the sound of their boots muffled by what remained of the snow. Wilson noticed a bald eagle watching them from the perch of a burnt snag, its eyes malevolent. Doug never saw it. He turned around to make conversation and Wilson was forced to sidestep and then dodge the aim of Doug's rifle.

"Damnit, Doug."

Doug halted and shifted his rifle skyward like a toy soldier.

"Give me the rifle."

"I swear I won't point it at you again."

"Just carry it over your shoulder like I showed you."

"But I want to be ready."

"Doug."

He slung it over his shoulder and they carried on side by side.

"So I wanted to apologize for telling you to fuck off the other day," Doug said.

He waited for a response, but Wilson kept his gaze fixed on the upper hillside.

"That was real shitty of me, brotha. You were just looking out for me is all. I see that. I get drinking and I'm not myself."

"Then stop drinking."

"See that's just what I've been thinking about. I've been giving it a lot of thought lately."

"Oh yeah."

"Really. But see, it's the bar that makes it so tough. Working there, running the place, hanging with the guys. Makes it real tough to stay dry."

"We all choose our lifestyle."

"But do we really choose it? Or does it choose us? It's like . . . Well, take Bethany for instance. I loved that girl. I still love that girl. She was the sweetest little thing. But after a couple years I just got bored of coming home to the same pussy every night. Couldn't help it."

Wilson finally turned to look at him. "For Pete's sake, Doug. You're talking about your son's mother."

"I know it. I know. I'm a dog. What can I say?"

He looked to Wilson for commiseration but none was forthcoming.

"I admire the kind of relationship you've got with Ellen. That seems like something real special. The whole high school sweetheart thing. That's great. But how . . . I mean, how have you made that work all this time?"

"I love her."

"And that's really enough?"

"Yes. It is."

"But don't you ever wonder what it would be like?"

"What's that?"

"To be with another woman."

Wilson turned to him with an eyebrow cocked.

"So that's the line, huh? Okay, brotha. I read you."

They came to a moderate incline and began laboring up the slope. Wilson watched the bald eagle drop from the snag and take off into a banking swoop across the road.

"Maybe I oughta start going to church."

"Maybe."

"Maybe I oughta . . ." Doug finally saw the bird as it was soaring away.

"Whoahoho. That was a big ass bald eagle, man! Did you see that?"

Late in the afternoon they arrived at one of Wilson's favorite hikes, a parklike timber patch that funneled downhill to the intersection of two logging roads. Wilson explained to Doug where to station himself below should the elk flush, and Doug hurried down the road and soon disappeared around the bend. When enough time had passed, Wilson unslung his rifle from across his back, cradled it with both hands at waist level, and walked into the forest.

The sun immediately vanished beneath the canopy, and the dark wild of that mature forest made him solemn and hyperaware. A monastic quiet presided here, and he became cognizant of his breathing. His thoughts ebbed empty. The smell was rich of damp soil and he began to focus on his footsteps, a slow heel to toe pace on ground soft with moss and wet leaves and pine needles. The world as real as it was ever going to be.

There was a small rivulet ahead somewhere. He could hear it soughing out of sight and he made that his bearing. He took a few dozen steps and then he could see the water slithering through the leaves like some liquid anaconda. Another noise brought the rifle to his shoulder. It was only a Douglas fir, swaying with the breeze and creaking like an old ship forever moored. He went on downhill as quietly as he was able, following the water and avoiding its marshy pools.

Soon he came upon a number of vine maples clothed in green hides of moss, the broadest of the lot supporting a deer stand some craftsman hunter had erected twenty feet up the trunk. The stand was now mossed over and rotting with disuse, and Wilson wondered why such industriousness had been abandoned. He took hold of the guide rope and imagined climbing the spikes that wound their way around the tree like a spiral staircase. He was testing his weight on the bottom spike when he heard the crack of a branch.

He let the rope back gently and readied his rifle as he peered into a thicket and the wooded knoll beyond. Instinct told him to wait so he stayed still beneath the deer stand, his breath as shallow as he could manage. He was about to move on when he noticed a bull elk sauntering toward him.

It was a massive dream of a beast and approaching at an angle obstructed by alder trees. Wilson could not make an exact tally of the long antler tines, but there were certainly more than enough. He concealed himself almost fully behind the maple tree and prayed the bull wouldn't pick up his scent as it came shuffling along. When the bull was nearly abreast of him, it stopped and lifted its head, displaying a fine black mane, its neck muscular from fights and conditioning. Wilson thought he might fire, but the foliage was simply too thick. He remained quiet, frozen in place. He would only get one chance.

When the bull turned to gaze downhill, Wilson began to stalk from tree to tree for a clearer shot. He felt lucky to have the white noise of the water to help cover the rustle of his steps. The bull remained unflinching and seemingly fixated. Wilson was beginning to taste him now. He needed just a few more steps when a chipmunk commenced chattering overhead. Wilson paused behind a tree. He gazed up and spotted the tiny striped rodent perched upon a high branch. Wilson put his finger to his lips and continued his ambush. The chipmunk chirped all the louder. It seemed to relish the opportunity, lunging into its cries like something ardent to the end.

The bull still did not stir. As Wilson took his last steps, the chipmunk began leaping from one branch to another in shrill pursuit. Wilson was bringing his gun to his shoulder when the chipmunk issued its most urgent alarm. The bull turned and spied his pursuer and was gone in an instant. There was a brief crash from the gully as the bull fled and then only the sound of the creek and the chipmunk utterly relentless.

Wilson raised his gun at the ball of orange fur and blasted. He saw what he took to be a puff of carnage and was satisfied to only hear the water once more. He began picking his way back across the creek when the chipmunk started up again. It wasn't a giggle, but that was the sound it made. Wilson slung his rifle over his shoulder and hiked out onto the road.

Lunchtime found them at a turnout along a main arterial. Louanne and the sheriff sat on the tailgate of the Chevy, and Wilson and Doug atop a small log they'd dragged into place. The sun was high and surprisingly warm, and they listened to songbirds as they ate ham sandwiches, fruit and oatmeal cookies.

They were just finishing their meal when a blue Dodge pickup came around the roadbend with its shocks squabbling. Soon the pickup came to a stop alongside them. The driver was so fat his stomach rested on the steering wheel, his cheeks so loaded with flesh they made him squint and gave him a look of everlasting jolly.

"Howdy, Sheriff," the man said. "Deputy Wilson."

"Any luck there, Bubba," the sheriff called.

"Jumped a few deer. That's about all."

Bubba was smiling like a blind man, waiting for a story. Wilson told him about his failed pursuit and Bubba chuckled often. His was a blithe world.

"I'm told there's some nice bulls running together up by the water tower," Bubba offered generously. "I couldn't find 'em, but that's where they're at, I hear."

The sheriff glanced at his watch. "It's only noon and you're already giving up?"

"The wife's home sick as a dog. She's pissed that I'm out here at all. Well. Good luck, fellas. Ma'am."

Bubba gave a little salute and drove on down the road, his Dodge slumped to the driver's side like it had a flat tire.

As Wilson watched Bubba go he seemed to be having a debate with himself. Finally, he cleared his throat. "Say, Louanne. I've been meaning to ask you something about Ellen."

She looked up from where she'd been tidying the lunch things and wore a patient look.

"It's just that she's still real worried about me, you know, just doing my job. I thought she'd sort of gotten past that but . . . well, I was wondering if there was anything that helped to comfort you when you thought Les might not make it home safe some nights."

She reflected for a time. Doug reached for another cookie while the sheriff picked at his nails with a pocket knife.

"Maybe I shouldn't have brought this up," Wilson said.

"Oh, it's okay, dear. I understand perfectly. Who better to ask, right?"

"I just wondered if you might know something I could say to her. Something that'd help ease her mind a bit."

"Unfortunately, there's nothing that you can say to Emma that'll make her not worry about you. That's just being human."

Wilson glanced to the sheriff who had looked up at Louanne.

"Being a cop is a dangerous job," Louanne continued. "But being a cop's wife is the worst of all. It must have taken me ten years before I finally got comfortable with the idea that I might have to raise our children alone one day. Emma will come around. It just takes time."

"You mean, Ellen," the sheriff said.

"That's what I said. Ellen."

"You said, Emma."

Louanne's brow creased with confusion and then she just looked angry. "No, I didn't."

I t was nearly nightfall and the woods were smoke blue and eerie. The sheriff drove as he and Wilson discussed the merits of bow hunting. Neither of them had fired a shot at an elk that day, and it wouldn't be long before it was too dark to do so.

The sheriff glanced in the rearview mirror. He tapped Wilson absently with the back of his hand. "Look at these two."

Wilson gave the backseat a look. Louanne and Doug were both napping, their heads bobbing with the road like sailors at sea. "At least—"

"There's elk," the sheriff called.

Four bulls had come down off the embankment and were trotting across the road. They looked like mythical creatures the way their hides seemed made of fog, and each of them sported a decent rack of horns. Gun in hand, Wilson was out of the vehicle before it had even stopped. He was raising up his rifle as the sheriff blew the cow call and issued two bleats. The mimicry made one bull pause and Wilson fired. The bull coughed and its forelegs buckled. Wilson was reloading and the sheriff was getting out of the truck as the bull struggled to its hooves and plunged down off the roadbank.

Wilson and the sheriff hurried over and found where the snow had been stained with gouts of the elk's blood. They followed a crimson trail for a few yards and then peered down a precipitous ravine all tangled and grown over with ferns and salal and what else they couldn't tell for it was a long dusky way to the bottom.

"Son of a bitch," said Wilson.

"It was a good shot."

"I hit him low in the lungs."

"Yeah, but you hit him."

"You can't even tell what's down there."

"I'm pretty sure there's a creek that runs along at the base of this."

"And then what?"

The sheriff leaned over the ledge and rocked back to flat footed. "Well, my boy. We're about to find out."

"Son of a bitch."

Doug was just climbing his way out of the cab and he walked over and stood among them. "What happened?"

"We hit a grizzly bear," Wilson said as he began walking back to the truck.

Doug went and bent over the blood. He looked back at the sheriff for confirmation.

"He shot a nice bull," said the sheriff.

"Then what's his problem?"

"Wasn't a kill shot. Bull made it over the edge and is somewhere down in that shit there. Now we have to go find it."

"Tonight?"

"Tom and me. You stay here with your grandmother."

"Come on, Pops. I wanna help."

"We're just going to get the head and leave some scent to keep the coyotes off him. You can help us pack him out tomorrow if you want."

At the truck Wilson was already making up a pack with flashlights, rope, knives, a bone saw, and a few candy bars. Louanne hadn't yet moved from the backseat and the sheriff came over and rested his hand on her knee.

"We've gotta dress it out tonight," the sheriff said. "Otherwise the meat won't be worth a darn."

"I know."

"I've told Doug to stay here and keep you company."

"Whatever you think is best."

"Are you feeling alright?"

"Oh. Just a little groggy."

"The old nap hangover, huh?"

She nodded.

"Could you pass me my compass there, dear."

Louanne lifted the antique wayfinder out of the cup holder and set it in his palm. He clasped the compass and her hand at the same time and flashed her a mischievous grin that was youthful as a Boy Scout.

"Aren't you gonna try and talk me out of this?"

"Would it do any good?"

He chuckled.

"I'll keep the truck warm for you guys."

Wilson tied the rope off to a sturdy cedar and then led the way down the ravine. He was snaking the rope from tree to tree as he went and tracking the blood the best he could. The sheriff followed close behind and their talk consisted of which steps to take and what things to watch for. There was very little snow beneath the canopy but the flora was slick and the way was steep and they were both slipping and using the rope to catch themselves. The sheriff moved stiffly and cautiously and he was as slow as one would expect an old man to be. With every minute the woods were dimming and it wouldn't be long before they'd need their flashlights to continue. When Wilson came to a giant nurse log, he stopped and waited for the sheriff, who soon came huffing up beside him.

"I can hear the creek," the sheriff said between labored gasps. "It can't be much farther."

"We're about to run out of light."

"Then we'd better get moving."

"Are you going to be able to climb back up this ravine?"

The sheriff looked up the slope as though he'd just realized what he'd committed himself to. "Hell, I used to sprint up hills like this."

"And I used to wear diapers."

The sheriff cackled. "You're a strapping lad. You can just pack me out if things go sideways. Look. You can even see the water running down there."

"And what if our bull's not lying down next to the creek?"

"Then I'm a horse's ass. Now come on and boost me over this stinking log."

They were just getting up the side of the tree when they heard branches cracking and foliage swooshing and the tromping of clumsy footsteps. They turned and watched Doug making his way down along the rope.

"Oh, joy," said Wilson.

"He'd better have something real good to say."

They leaned against the nurse log and crossed their arms and waited for him. Doug moved down the slope like a drunk on the final inch of a bottle of tequila. As he approached he suddenly pitched backwards and completed his descent as if he were sliding into home plate. He stood up swatting the soil from his backside.

"You just decided to leave your grandmother sitting up there in the dark by herself," the sheriff said.

"She told me I ought to come along with you guys if that's what I wanted."

"So then you just decided that you didn't need to listen to me?"

"I didn't mean any disrespect, Pops."

"Well, that's just exactly what it feels like."

"Pops—"

"Hush now, Douglas! We don't have time to waste horsing around."

"Pops—"

"You wanted to leave your grandmother alone so you could come participate. Great. You can carry the head back up to the truck."

Doug seemed properly chastised and fixed his eyes on the ground. After a time he glanced at Wilson to see if there lay any sympathy with him, but Wilson had already turned to help the sheriff atop the log. He had his hands underneath the sheriff's rump and was heaving him upward.

"I can help," Doug said.

He stepped forward and reached to lend a hand, but the sheriff had already planted his feet and swung out of range.

"Looks pretty easy on this side," the sheriff called. "I'm going over."

Wilson and Doug shared a look.

"He's my grandpa, you know."

"Then you'd think you'd listen to him better."

There was just the scantest of light remaining when they finally reached the creek. Their track of blood dribbled right up to the water's edge and it was clear that the bull had gone across. The creek itself was only twenty feet wide but it was running rapidly and the water was very cold. It was impossible to tell how deep. Up to their knees perhaps. Maybe deeper. Here and there in the stream rocks stood up out of the water, some of them still glazed with snow. They took a minute to study, but there was no sign of the bull.

"You think he's over there?" Wilson asked the sheriff.

"I think if I was him I wouldn't have the will to start back up that next slope tonight. Especially not with my lungs bleeding."

"You think we can all make it across the creek without falling in?"

"At this point I think we'd be pansies not to try."

By the glow of their flashlights they found half a dozen rocks which, added together, made a plausible footbridge. Wilson went first, and other than one long precarious stride with the frigid water sucking at his boots, it was an easier crossing than it looked. The sheriff went next, and with Wilson's help he tottered across, followed by Doug. They spread out and began searching the creekside.

They had nearly given up when the sheriff found him. The bull had wedged itself beneath a fallen tree and the quarter-ton creature stared at the flashlight with one eye. He was barely breathing and he appeared uninterested in struggling any further.

"Here he is," the sheriff said, a touch of somberness to his voice.

He pulled out his forty-five caliber Smith and Wesson and shot the bull once in the back of the head, the sound swallowed up by the creek. The elk looked much the same as it had, only now it wasn't breathing. Either way it was a magnificent animal and the sheriff stood there and admired it until Wilson came over and dropped his pack on the pebbly bank. He removed a knife and the bone saw and held them up to the light.

"Which do you want to take care of first?"

Thirty minutes later they were picking their way back across the creek, first Wilson, then the sheriff, then Doug swinging the elk's severed head by one antler. It appeared that Doug might fall or vomit at any moment. The sheriff landed on the creekbank and turned and watched his grandson.

"Do not drop that head in the creek," he said.

"How can it be so heavy?"

"Pack a ribcage and then tell me what's heavy."

Doug was stepping from one rock to another when the antler started slipping through his fingers. He dropped to one knee and caught the head in his lap, slowly realizing how covered he was in gore.

"He might pass out," Wilson said.

"He drops that head, he's walking home."

Doug reached down and doubled his grip on the antlers and then moved forward holding the head out in front of himself with both hands like a demented pagan involved in some overly convoluted ritual. When he finally reached the opposite bank he set the head on the ground, wiped his bloody hands down the front of his pants, and looked up the ravine.

"I should have stayed in the truck."

The ravine seemed twice as steep returning, and it was a slow and tedious way to go. Several times they had to rest and catch their breath. Wilson kept asking how the sheriff was faring and he answered in monosyllables or not at all, clinging to the rope as though it were his own limb. Wilson offered to carry the head and Doug took the pack and they trudged on. A light rain began pattering upon the canopy above.

Doug reached the road first and they heard him murmur a few choice profanities. A moment later Wilson resurfaced followed by the sheriff close behind. Wilson dropped the head to the ground and it thumped and rolled still. They looked up and down the road, an empty and foreboding blackness in each direction with the rain picking up and no truck and no Louanne and a long way from home. Wilson felt his stomach knot something nautical and his mind began playing through a series of possibilities. He looked to the sheriff and the look returned was one he'd like to have done without. Fear and fury just barely contained.

"Oh, boy," Doug groaned.

Wilson took a step between them by way of mediation. "There's got to be a good explanation for this."

"And what would that be?" the sheriff asked.

"Well, let's just take a minute to come up with it."

The sheriff wouldn't even look at his grandson. Doug kept pacing around and shining his flashlight aimlessly. After five minutes they'd still not plotted a palatable explanation for why Louanne and the truck were missing.

"There's no way she would have just left us out here," the sheriff said.

Wilson tried not to let on how thoroughly he agreed. "Any minute we're gonna see those old headlights and she's gonna drive up with a story we never would've even thought of."

The rain wasn't letting up and the three of them went and stood under the best sheltering tree they could find. They waited another thirty minutes and remained mostly in silence. Despite the tree, their clothes were beginning to saturate and the night was turning cold.

"How long do you think we can stand here before we get hypothermia?" Doug asked.

Both Wilson and the sheriff looked at him and turned away without comment. As loath as they were to admit it, they'd each been wondering the same thing.

"She'll come back for us," Wilson said.

"She might," the sheriff said. Then after a long pause, "Or she might not."

"It's your call."

"Let's give her another ten minutes and then let's walk."

They gave her fifteen and then they gathered their things and began taking the road downhill. Wilson carried the elk's head, its tongue lolling out the side of its mouth. It would not stop raining. They tried to walk under the trees for a while, but it made the way more difficult and they weren't convinced it was keeping them any drier so they just resigned themselves to the center of the road and walked on. And on. They'd traveled maybe two miles when Doug finally asked how much farther.

"To where?" the sheriff answered.

"The nearest house."

The sheriff thought about it. "Maybe fifteen miles."

"Seriously?"

"Yeah."

"We're screwed."

"It could be a lot better."

Time seemed endless, the forest and the road and the darkness the same. They'd walked another five miles when they started shivering and they began to think less about Louanne and more about their own beleaguering prospects. They decided to eat their candy bars and it gave them a brief jolt and then they felt worse than before. The sheriff began to look haggard and his respiration was sounding awful. Wilson kept expecting the old man to drop and he wondered how far they would be able to carry him. He was ready to forsake the antlers and leave the head where it lay when they saw headlights approaching from the way they'd come. They waved enormously and a VW station wagon came to a stop alongside them. Alone in the car was a teenage boy. He rolled down the window.

"Boy, am I glad I spotted you guys. I've been driving around lost for hours."

"We're pretty happy to see you too," said Wilson.

"Say, what happened to your rig?"

"We don't know yet."

Once they were all loaded they peeled off their outer layers and persuaded the boy to blast the heat as high as it would go. Waylon Jennings crooned from the eight track player and the boy was full of inventive theories about what might have happened to Louanne.

The sheriff directed him on to his house and they turned up the driveway with great anticipation. Around the corner they came and there was the sheriff's red Chevy parked in front of the house.

"You don't have two trucks like that, do you?" the boy asked.

"No, I don't," the sheriff said.

The boy looked troubled. "Gee. I don't even know what I'd do if somebody had left me out there in the woods like that. You coulda been in real trouble if I hadn't driven up."

The sheriff exited without a word.

"Well, thank you, Donny," Wilson said.

"Ah, that's alright," the boy said.

Wilson and Doug followed the sheriff into the house. The lights were all on and the radio was playing and it smelled of taco meat. One by one they looked into the kitchen. Louanne was in her apron and she giggled about something on the radio. She turned and saw them standing there.

"Well, I'll be. Dougie *and* Tom. I'll need to fix something extra I guess." The sheriff seemed unsurprised.

"The three of you look wet as muskrats. Where you all been?"

"Louanne," the sheriff said. "We've been out in the woods waiting for you."

"Waiting for me? Why. I've been here all day waiting for you."

Doug's mouth went agape and he aimed it at Wilson. The sheriff just walked on into the den and Louanne watched him go.

"What's the matter with him?" she said.

Doug stepped into the kitchen. "Nana. Don't you remember going hunting today?"

She frowned as she strained to recall.

"We all went hunting together. All four of us. Don't you remember?"

"Well now, hold on a second. I'm misremembering." She had let go of the pan and the meat was starting to smell burnt.

"Tom shot a bull."

"He did? He did. That's right. He did."

"And then you and I were waiting for them in the truck and you told me to go on and help if that's what I wanted to do."

"Yep. Yep. That's right."

"But why did you drive off, Nana?"

"Well I . . ." She was looking around for clues and noticed the pan on the stove. "I had to get some supper ready for you boys."

"But Nana. There was just the one truck. You left us stranded out there."

She snapped a finger at him. "Now cut it out, Douglas. I don't appreciate you criticizing me when here I am cooking supper for you. I can't be expected to be your chauffer and your cook all at the same time, can I?"

"But Nana . . ."

Wilson had taken ahold of his elbow. He pointed at the stove. "That meat looks like it might be about ready, Louanne. Looks tasty too."

Louanne seemed to really see her cooking for the first time since they'd arrived. She quickly raised the pan and flipped the burner off, muttering something inaudible as she stirred the burnt meat in with the rest.

"Sure do appreciate you cooking," Wilson continued. "I'll probably just take one taco myself. How about you, Doug?"

"I guess I'll take one too," he mumbled.

While Louanne dished up the plates, Wilson and Doug went looking for the sheriff and found him in his leather chair drinking a glass of straight bourbon. He waved his arm haphazardly, motioning for them to help themselves to the bar. They stayed where they were and waited for the sheriff to speak. Finally, he said, "I'm sorry, boys."

"Hardly your fault," said Wilson.

"It is though. It is my fault. The warning signs have all been there but I've just been hoping beyond hope that I'd been reading them wrong. Douglas, I especially owe you an apology. I should have been explaining things to you but I didn't want to trouble you until I was sure."

"But what's going on, Pops? Does she have dementia or something?"

"Alzheimer's, I suspect."

"How long have you known?"

"I guess I knew for absolute certain the moment I saw our Chevy parked in the driveway just now. When did it start? It's hard to say. Some months ago. At first it seemed like forgetfulness, distractedness, I don't know what. Looking back, I can pick out all these little situations that I might have attributed it to, but at the time I just kept thinking . . . I just kept thinking . . . Huh. Denial can be an awfully powerful thing."

"So what do you do, Pops?"

"That sure is the question."

The sheriff took a sip of bourbon. He looked off toward the kitchen and straight back at his lap. Wilson and Doug turned and saw Louanne standing timid against the doorjamb. She looked very scared and not one of them had any idea what there was to say.

II

I was never afraid of the mountain like a lot of the other guys who worked out there were. I'm not trying to boast about it, but I wasn't. I guess I didn't see what good it did being afraid. There wasn't anything anyone could do to stop it. And I wasn't liable to find another job that was gonna pay me half as good as hauling those logs out of those woods.

At that point I'd been with Weyerhaeuser for sixteen years. I'd worked my way up to a faller until some jackass, I won't say his name, managed to drop a tree on me and break my back. Now I just drive. Like I was that day.

I remember it being a dark afternoon with lots of ash falling. The crews were cutting up on the northwest side of the mountain and they were running through sawblades like crazy. The ash and the grit would just eat those blades up. I believe they were cutting three or four miles away from the crater and I know that sounds awfully close, but at the time we were assured that we were in absolutely no danger. That we'd be alerted should there be any sign of an eruption and evacuated to high ground.

Of course, that all turned out to be a bunch of malarkey. If we'd been there when it blew, we would've been incinerated. The only thing that saved us was that it blew on a Sunday. Though that didn't save some of the gyppos. I blame the scientists for it. They wouldn't give anybody a straight answer.

Anyways, on this particular day about a week or two before the blast they loaded me up with a few logs and I started heading back to Longview. I kept calling out on the radio making sure the road was clear. But even so I was always hyper alert at that time because there were all these moron city types out there sneaking around the roadblock and getting in our way. And sure enough, I came around a tight corner and there's a vehicle stopped in the middle of the road and a guy sitting in the driver seat with a map covering up the inside of the windshield.

If you've ever hauled a full load of timber down a five or six percent grade then you know you can't stop that sucker on a dime. I had about one second to decide if I was going to smash into this guy or go into the ditch and I chose the latter. I didn't even have time to lay on the horn.

That sure was a rollicking ride. I had two tires on the road and two in the ditch and I was just praying that I didn't run out of ditch. Some of the tires were blowing and the load was clanging and banging around behind me. At one point I just about rolled the rig over on its side, which I do believe would have been the end of me.

Finally, I got the rig stopped down at the bottom of the hill. First thing I did was get on the radio and call for help. Then I jumped out of the cab and proceeded to run right up to that sonofabitch. Asked him what the hell he thought he was doing stopped in the middle of the road like that. He told me he was lost. He was looking for Spirit Lake and made a wrong turn somewhere. And then he starts pointing at his map and rattling off road numbers like I was just there to assist him with directions.

Boy that pissed me off. That really got me heated. I told him in no uncertain terms that if I or any of my crew ever caught him driving on Weyerhaeuser roads again that we would chain him to a tree and beat the living sap out of him. He didn't have anything more to say after that. He just got into his vehicle and drove back to the highway. And I never did see him again. Not until I saw his picture on the television.

H alf asleep and grumbling through his hangover, Wilson slogged up the sheriff's office stairs and turned into the briefing room. Seated at the table was a bellysome deputy with a bushy mustache and a red drunkard's face. He looked up from his newspaper and doughnuts and shook his head grinning.

"Someone got a little too jolly last night," said the deputy.

"My outlaw uncle wouldn't leave me alone with his moonshine," said Wilson.

"Yeah, you don't look great."

"What could I do? The whole fam damily was at our house till after one."

"Get some food in you and you'll straighten out. Hey, you seen our tree yet?"

Wilson fixed himself a cup of coffee, grabbed a doughnut, and then went over and had a look at the artificial Christmas tree wrapped in twinkling bulbs. He leaned in and saw how someone had ornamented the tree with cutout pictures of wanted criminals and other infamous hoodlums and miscreants indigenous to their district. Wilson took some time to peruse the glaring and deranged mugshots drooping from various plastic boughs. Most of them he recognized. The local pedophile, the arsonist, several wife beaters. A man with no eyebrows and a sly satanic leer. Another with a skull like a battering ram and murderousness plainly visible. Monsters. Men to confront in dark alleys alone.

Wilson took a long draught of his coffee and asked, "Tell me again why we do this job?"

The deputy slowly folded up his newspaper. "Cause it feels pretty dang good to wrap those pricks up and throw 'em in a box."

"You've got the holiday spirit."

"I really do love busting these assholes on Christmas. Fills me with joy."

Wilson refilled his coffee and took another doughnut. "I'd better sober up before the sarge gets in."

"He's already here. He's waiting for you in the office with the newbie."

Wilson kneaded his forehead and groaned.

"Merry Christmas."

When Sergeant Davies saw him coming, he stood up behind his desk and said, "Here he is."

The young rookie seated across from him rose and turned with a stiff swiftness and waited to see what he was supposed to do next. He was a remarkably handsome man, hair golden and wavy, teeth like pearls, eyes vivid and glacier blue. Overall, he looked like some Greek hero refabricated from Midwest origins and cornfed into physical perfection. A cop that criminals would hate.

"This is Steve Sheffield," the sergeant announced. "He's coming to us straight from the academy."

The rookie stuck out his hand. "Hey, it's a pleasure to meet you."

Wilson sized him up as they shook. "You sure you wouldn't rather be an underwear model?"

The rookie laughed easily. "Ah, no way. I've been wanting to be a cop for too long."

"How'd you get roped into training on Christmas?"

He looked to the sergeant for help.

"Henry's got some family affairs to settle back east. He'll be taking a leave of absence, so we need Sheffield here up to speed as soon as we can manage. Sit. Sit."

All three of them settled into their chairs. The sergeant was appraising Wilson.

"Tom, you look like you were guzzling eggnog last night."

"I wish it had just been eggnog."

The sergeant rolled his eyes and directed himself to the rookie. "This is where I tell you to keep some things to yourself. Well. I'm not going to belabor all the official mumbo jumbo I'm supposed to go through with you right now. It was supposed to be my day off and I've got to get back home to play Santa for the grandkids. Wilson will cover all the basics. We'll answer some questions tomorrow. Etcetera, etcetera."

"I'll bet you fill out that Santa suit pretty nicely," Wilson said.

"I didn't hear that. Now there was something else. Ahh, yes."

The sergeant removed a file from among one of the stacks of papers cluttering his desk and passed it to Wilson who took a minute to scan the first document, a lengthy rap sheet filled with drug offenses, assaults, and a smattering of minor robberies. He flipped the page and began looking over a series of pictures depicting the felon. A large disheveled fellow with a powerful brow and eyes set deep and bizarrely close together. In every photo he appeared disinterested, like a Neanderthal just woken from a nap. Wilson passed the file to the rookie.

"Griswold Frye," the sergeant said. "Everybody used to call him Griz. He's been in the state pen for the last eight years. Should have been twice that but the prosecutor turned into a bleeding-heart liberal so here we are again. Griz is a local boy, born and raised in the boonies. He and I used to battle some back when I was still a deputy. Sheriff Jenkins got to know him quite well."

"So, he's back in the area?"

"He's back."

"Where's he staying?"

"He's supposed to be living with his brother down on Hoag Street. I doubt that he is. We've already received one call that he's muscling in on our local pushers."

"How long has he been out?"

"About a week."

"Doesn't like to waste time."

"The thing you need to know about Griz is that he likes to beat on authorities. That's what finally landed him in the slammer as long as it did. He absolutely uncorked on a security guard who caught him stealing down in Brush Prairie. I won't show you the pictures. And the other thing to remember about him is that he's not nearly as stupid as he looks. You just take extra care around him until we figure out what he's up to. And as soon as we do figure it out we'll call in the whole brigade and ship him back to Walla Walla where he belongs."

"Griswold Frye," Wilson said. He turned to Sheffield. "You sure you're ready for this, rookie?"

"I've been waiting for it my whole life."

"One broken nose and that face of yours won't look so pretty."

"I'm ready when you are."

Soon after sunrise Wilson took the rookie on a tour of the district which he would soon share. It was a mild-weathered Tuesday and there was even some sunshine on this holiday morning. The country roads were even more empty than usual, and the homes they passed looked snug and festive with many chimneys smoking.

Wilson was explaining which roads to remember first and where they connected and all along he pointed out each house and business and briar patch that had contained some degree of trouble. Like every policeman, his mental map was formed of experience and waymarked with memories, drawn for others through the telling of tales, each of them true as the last all the way down to the grisliest particulars. Nothing unspeakable for a cop. Only the world as it is and must be understood in order to survive.

Late in the morning they pulled into the Trading Post parking lot in Yacolt. Across the street was the primary school and a family was already out in the recess field rigging up some gift of a toy rocket. Wilson shut off the engine.

"So where are you from, Sheffield? Say, you mind if I just call you Shef?"

The rookie shrugged and said, "I'm from Everett."

"City boy, huh?"

"Pretty much."

"You ever spend much time in the country?"

"Not really. Always liked hiking and camping though."

Wilson popped a couple aspirin and washed them down with a bottle of water. "Well, the first thing you need to realize is that most of the folks around here have no patience for anybody with big city pretensions. These folks are country, with a capital C. They're not interested in granola or punk rock. Most of them can't afford to shop at REI, and if they're hiking it's not to take a picture in front of some pretty waterfall. They hike when they're working or hunting."

"Okay."

"You've got to try and match their mentality or you'll get nowhere. The last new guy that tried to work down here got chewed up and spit out so fast it made Sergeant Davies' head spin. It's gonna take some time for folks to learn to trust you, but they'll come around once they realize that you're honest and respectful. When I first started working out here I handed out a business card to every person I could. I shook their hands, tried my best to learn their names. I must have gone through four boxes of business cards. Our secretary couldn't figure out what I kept needing them for. She's got the city mentality.

"People like her don't realize that I'm a long ways away from the nearest deputy. There's gonna be lots of times when you won't have backup for twenty minutes. Think about that. You're just one guy. That's a long time to be on your own if things really start going badly. There's places in this district where your radio might not even work at all. So if you've got the citizens on your side, then they can help keep you out of trouble. And there's an awful lot you can learn from them if you're willing to pay attention."

"How long have you worked out here?"

"Three years."

"Is this where you started?"

"No. I started out on the north side of Vancouver."

"Why'd you transfer?"

"I was banished."

"Banished?"

"I called my lieutenant out for being a liar in front of our entire department."

"Why?"

"Because he was lying about me. I'll tell you about it some other time. This district was supposed to be my punishment."

"Do you wish you could go back?"

"I've already had the chance and I turned it down. The ones that were trying to move me back couldn't believe that I wanted to stay out here. They're terrified of this area. They think the bogeyman's gonna get them. I told them they were all afraid of the dark."

Shef was chuckling. "What if I'm afraid of the dark?"

"You'll either get over it or you'll quit."

"So you really like it out here?"

"I do. There's a lot of good people that live out here. They work hard. They love the land. And they need us."

Shef was watching Wilson and waiting for him to continue but Wilson was looking straight through the windshield. The family had figured out how their rocket worked and it was just fizzing into a sluggish takeoff. The children craned their necks to watch it fly.

"A couple years ago a little girl was abducted from this very spot," Wilson continued. "It was after school. Someone loaded her into a van and drove off without anybody noticing. The whole town searched for her for weeks and weeks, but nothing turned up. It started to seem hopeless. Then one day I went to go check on a guy who'd molested a couple children about ten years back. It's just a routine thing we do. Make sure he's still living at the same address, poke around a little bit. Nothing ever comes of it. In fact, some of the other deputies had just been there the week before.

"So I get to the guy's house which wasn't far from here and he was just as friendly as could be. His house was clean, he's got pictures of angels and crosses on his wall. He's got pay stubs showing he's been working as a janitor. Everything looks good. Shipshape. But I just got this feeling like something there wasn't right. I didn't know what it was, but I started walking around his house a little bit and I could sense the guy was starting to get uncomfortable. I asked him if I could take a look down in his cellar. And he just froze. That's when I knew."

"He had her down there?"

"She was okay. She's back with her family now. In the fourth grade and doing well."

Shef was silent. Wilson waited for him to play out the scene vicariously. When he was finished, he said, "That's really intense, man."

"You're gonna see things you never thought were possible. And then you're gonna see them again in your sleep. You need to forget right now everything you thought a human being was supposed to be like when you were growing up in the suburbs. The bad guys are out there. They don't always look or act like you think they would. And they want what they're not supposed to have."

Shef reflected for a moment and then asked, "Do you ever get scared out here?"

Wilson began to reply when the radio crackled with their first call of the day, a burglary on Cedar Creek Road. Wilson confirmed the dispatch and began heading west.

"Something like this always happens on Christmas," Wilson said. "Get your pen and pad ready. I wanna see how you are at taking notes."

The residence was set back away from the road in a densely-wooded neighborhood shaded most of the day by a blend of conifers. The home was newly-constructed and wrapped with a deck. In the yard was a swing set and an assortment of wheeled toys. Wilson parked at the top of the drive and, trailed by Shef, he stepped up onto the porch and knocked twice on the front door.

A small dog began yapping and scratching at the inside of the door, and a man wearing a Rudolph the Reindeer sweater soon swung it open, brushing the terrier aside with his foot. "Knock it off now, Tinkerbell. These are the good guys," he told the dog. "Thank you for coming, officers. Boy, did we wake up to a surprise."

Behind the man on a rug, two young boys, apparently twins, were playing with Lincoln Logs and payed little attention to the officers. To their side was a grand Christmas tree and below it a mess of presents and wrapping paper. A woman entered from the kitchen bearing two cups of warm cider and passed them to the deputies. The man gestured toward the tree.

"The boys were the first to notice what happened. It was pretty late in the morning as I don't usually get to sleep in. Patricia and I were just getting out of bed when the boys ran into our room and starting shouting that someone had already opened all of our presents. At first, I thought they were fibbing as usual. Figured they'd gotten overanxious and were trying to dodge the blame. But then we seen the muddy bootprints on the deck, and since I don't have boots like that I knew they were telling the truth about it."

Shef was scribbling notes while Wilson walked over and had a look under the tree.

"How many of the presents were opened?" he asked.

"Every single one of them."

"And which ones were missing?"

"None of them. Not a one. Someone came in here and opened all of our dang presents and didn't take nothing."

"Yes, they did," the woman interjected.

"Well, yes they did take something. That's what I was just getting to. Whoever came in here this morning didn't steal none of the presents, but they did steal my gun. It was up on the mantle over there. Unloaded. It was always unloaded. And it was up where . . . Well look right there. That's where it was at, up on the mantle there where the boys couldn't even come close to getting to it. I mean, they're only three and a half. So that's how we know all of this couldn't have been them."

Wilson was looking everything over, Shef trailing him.

"We don't keep the door locked," the man said. "So there's that. Guess we'll have to start taking more precautions. Tinkerbell here certainly didn't do her job."

"Have you ever seen something like this?" the woman asked.

"No," Wilson said. "This would be a first."

"It's just so bizarre. To think that someone would stroll in here and open up every one of our presents while we were sleeping right upstairs. And then not to even bother taking nothing. That is, I mean, nothing except the gun."

"Do you have any idea who might have done this?"

"Geez. I can't imagine knowing someone who would do something like that. I'd say it's got to be some kind of a lunatic. I don't know how else to explain it."

Wilson finished up questioning the couple and evaluating the crime scene. He measured the bootprints and took some pictures and told them to leave things as they were until the detective arrived.

They had loaded up and were driving slowly along Cedar Creek Road looking for additional evidence when they noticed an aging woman waving at them from behind the window of her living room. Wilson pulled over to the shoulder of the road and waited. A moment later the woman came striding briskly down the drive. They got out to receive her.

"Merry Christmas, ma'am," Wilson said.

"Merry Christmas, officers." She looked at the rookie. "He must be a new one."

"First day," Shef said.

"And I thought your partner was the handsomest one around here. You look like you should be on one of them soap operas getting chased around by the women all day."

"Thank you, ma'am."

"Was there something you needed help with today?" Wilson asked.

"Well, I was gonna put in a call to the sheriff's office about it, but then I started feeling silly about it. But then I saw you rolling by all slowlike so I thought I'd tell ya that I saw a real weird looking fella running along the road early this morning. I'd say it was five thirty-five or so."

Wilson glanced at Shef who looked like he was having a major epiphany. Then he remembered his notepad and fluttered about readying himself once again.

"We're actually here in your neighborhood to investigate a burglary that occurred sometime early this morning," Wilson explained. "You may have seen our suspect fleeing the scene of the crime. Were you able to get a good look at him?"

"I was. I keep a couple lights on at the end of the drive for just such things, and I could see him pretty well. He was a bit younger than me. Maybe fifty or so. Very skinny, scrawny. Just wearing jeans and a flannel shirt or two. And he was bald. Mostly bald. It looked like he had one of them combover things going on when a guy starts getting real partial to the last few hairs he's got left to claim. Weird looking fella. Don't know him."

"And why didn't you call it in?"

"I woulda called. Well I shoulda called, but I didn't because I started thinking that maybe he was just one of those jogger guys. I don't really know what they look like. And adding to that he wasn't carrying nothing. Didn't seem like he had stolen nothing or nothing. Just thought maybe he was a jogger. Something strange like that."

"Well that's alright. I'm just trying to get your general impression is all. And which direction was he heading?"

"He was going that way. Westward."

"Alright. Anything else you can add?"

"Nope."

"Well, we thank you for your assistance. Enjoy the rest of your Christmas."

"I surely will."

They got back in the car and Wilson looked over the rookie's notes.

"So, you have any idea who it might be?" Shef asked.

"I know exactly who it is."

"Yeah?"

"Elmer Bugg."

"That's a real name?"

"Around here it is. Let's go see if we can find that gun."

The suspect's four-acre lot was a jungle of weeds and thistle and remnants of things nobody was ever going to need or want, including him. A rusted bedlam of bedsprings and hat racks, broken chains and bear traps, washtubs and bowling balls and rear axles to vehicles long extinct. So many curious artifacts with no apparent order or foreseeable use. And through it all, a grungy footpath leading to the trailer that sheltered such a revolting landlord. Just a little graying box of a home streaked with moss-colored grime and slouching unevenly upon wooden blocks that were rotting with the climate. The windows had all been busted out and patched back with cardboard and duct tape, and sloppily done at that. Some strange gutter was hanging by a single nail and dripped. Rooftop antennas seemed angled for random intergalactic communication. The door was just an old plastic sled and hinged with wire.

Wilson and Shef had been standing at the edge of the property, Shef's eyes alive like he was beholding some ruin of another time, perhaps the future. They took special care as they picked their way through that trash heap of a lawn, on guard against things that might bite or jab at them. Wilson took the first step up to the trailer and the wooden plank collapsed and he nearly pitched forward to his hands and knees. He decided to just holler.

"Elmer. It's the police. Come on out and have a chat with us."

They could hear his nasally indecipherable voice within the trailer, a shuffling of furniture.

"Come on out now. We just need to ask you some questions."

More sounds of movement. A cry like some cornered marsupial.

"We're coming in, Elmer. Don't give us any trouble."

Wilson drew his gun. Shef did the same. They nodded at each other and Wilson skipped to the second step and banged on the sled. The makeshift door was unlatched and Wilson flung it open and hurried inside with his gun poised.

Seated at a little card table with his back turned to them was Elmer. He wore a set of giant rubber ear muffs like those for doing yardwork, and he was hunched over and busy with some task like a goblin at his workbench. Elmer muttered to himself as something squealed down beneath his legs.

Shef followed Wilson into the trailer. They crept forward, guns at the ready, but still Elmer took no notice of them. They peered over Elmer's shoulder to see what he was working on, and found a beheaded mole flayed open on a bloody wooden board. Elmer was cutting at it with a dull knife.

"Good lord," Shef said.

Wilson hollered Elmer's name. There was no response, so he shouted it again even louder. Finally, he stomped on the floor a few times and Elmer turned and spasmed and tossed his knife up into the air.

"Don't shoot," he shouted as his knife clattered into the nearby sink.

"We're not gonna shoot you," Wilson said.

"What?"

"We're not gonna shoot you."

"What?"

"Take your damn earmuffs off!"

They watched him remove the earmuffs and then grab at his racing heart, the old loon wheezing through his ruined teeth. He was an improbably unattractive human, the few hairs on his head clinging to his scalp like wet cobwebs, his eyes overlarge and perpetually bloodshot, his ears pointed like some species of bat. A face that never knew love.

"I thought you was gonna shoot me for sure," he said.

"Elmer, what are you doing with that mole?" Wilson asked.

"The mole? Well. Shoot. I'm a little embarrassed about that."

"Were you planning on eating the mole?"

His eyes dropped to the floor. "Yeah, I was gonna add him to my stew."

"And what's in that sack beneath your legs?"

"Last night's catch. Coupla rats and some field mice."

"Don't you have any money for food?"

"I've got some change in the jar there, but it ain't much. Hard to find work, you know. Only real job I ever had was at the plywood mill and now that's closed. But I'm getting by. And the rodents really aren't all that bad to eat once you get used to 'em. Good a protein as any. Heck. In China that's all they eat."

"Why were you wearing the ear muffs?"

"Because I don't like to hear them squealing at me, of course. Would you?"

Wilson looked around Elmer's disgusting habitat. The couch was a sinkhole. The kitchen a collection of small travesties. The pantry lined with jars of viscous horribles.

"Elmer, we need to ask you a few questions," Wilson said.

"Alright, but what's this all about?"

"Deputy Sheffield and I are investigating an incident that occurred in this neighborhood earlier this morning. Can you tell us where you were between the hours of four and seven?"

"I was sleeping."

"You were sleeping the entire time?"

"You said between four and seven, right? Let me just double check. Yep. I was sleeping the whole time."

"So you weren't running along Cedar Creek Road this morning?"

"How the heck? I mean . . . Well, yes. That's right. I had been thinking of yesterday. This morning I had some traps to check. Dang cats and coons been cleaning me out if I don't get there extra early."

"I see."

"And I decided to run out and back for a bit of exercise."

"Uh huh."

"It's very important to get your exercise."

"And what were you doing before you were running along Cedar Creek Road?"

"Well, that's when I was sleeping."

Wilson glanced down. "Elmer, those boots of yours have seen better days. I could probably find some newer ones for you. Though I'll need your size. Do you mind if I just measure the length of your boot real quick?"

"That's alright. I'm content with these. Really, I'm . . ."

Wilson bent down and spread the tape out. Elmer avoided Shef's eye contact as he stood there twitching uncomfortably.

"Just hold still now, Elmer. I've nearly got it measured."

"Say, what sort of an incident are you investigating anyhow?"

"Ten and a half inches. Interesting. How about we try one more thing. Would you mind showing me the tread of your boots? That would go a long way toward helping us out."

"Well, I don't know what this is all about. I think there must be some kind of a mistake."

"Just turn your boot to the side for me."

"They're just my old boots is all," Elmer said as he was turning over his other foot.

Wilson clutched the shoe. "Isn't this strange."

All three of them looked down and saw a scrap of green wrapping paper stuck to the bottom of his boot with a piece of errant tape, a picture of Santa Claus torn in half. Elmer looked to Wilson, back to the boot, back to Wilson.

"Okay, but I never took nothing," Elmer said.

"Where's the gun?"

"Gun? There wasn't no gun in any of those boxes."

"We'll have to search your trailer." Wilson looked around at the filth and the rancid squalor. "The detective will have to search your trailer."

"I never saw no gun. I didn't take nothing. I swear to that."

"You think we can trust you?"

"I'll swear to it. On the Bible. On my mother. I can take a lie detector test even. I swear it. I never took nothing. I just wanted to have a Christmas this year."

The sadness of that statement hung in the air for several moments.

"Elmer?" Wilson said.

"What?"

"I don't know. Come on. We've gotta take you in to the station."

"Ahhh. What am I gonna do? I ain't even finished butchering the meat yet."

Wilson shook his head. "Come on, Elmer. If we hurry up we can get you a turkey dinner at the jailhouse."

"Oh yeah? Should I take my medications now?"

"Let's grab all the medications you've got. Now go on and dump those rats out in the yard."

"What about the field mice?"

"Those too."

T hat lackluster day after Christmas, when the spirit of the season has been spent. Wilson and Shef were back at it again, tidying up messes spilling over from the previous day. Domestic affairs mostly. Guerilla wars fought over small children. Petty battles to determine the rightful owner of some toaster oven or box of dusty records.

The deputies lost most of their afternoon to an inane family dispute arising from a bag of cat food and devolving into a dozen unassociated threads of bitterness. They left the house exhausted and famished and ate a late lunch at Dolores' place. Afterwards, they were heading back toward their squad car when Wilson nodded at a hefty man just lumbering out of his maroon Wagoneer.

"I want you to meet this guy," Wilson said. "Just give him a chance to talk if he's in the mood. You'll learn a few things."

They walked across the parking lot, and as the man noticed them he smiled and offered his huge bear paw of a hand.

"This is Ferlin Blackstone," Wilson told the rookie. "He's our local author."

"Right on," Shef said. "I've never met a real author."

At this the woodsman writer seemed to glow. "I'm no Hunter S.

Thompson, but I'm starting to get recognized. Tom here's been one of my most loyal readers. You must have all five of my books by now."

"I've got 'em all."

"What do you write about?" Shef asked.

"I like to dabble, but my bread and butter is Sasquatch. That's Bigfoot to the layman."

"Bigfoot! So you write fictional stuff."

"No. I generally stick to the facts."

"You mean, about how it's all a big urban legend?"

A massive frown overwhelmed Ferlin's face. He turned to Wilson. "You must not have explained much to him yet."

"I wanted you to do it."

Shef's glance bounced between Wilson and Ferlin. "You guys actually believe in Bigfoot?"

"Got nothing to do with belief," Ferlin said. "They inhabit this country. Simple as that. You aren't busy right now are you, Tom?"

"No. Go ahead."

"Excellent." He cleared his throat. "Well, the first thing you need to realize is that the government is keeping the truth from us because they don't think the populace can handle it. And they're probably right about that. Just look at yourself. The truth of it is that bounty hunters have been trying to covertly eliminate the Sasquatches from the state of Washington for some time. Unfortunately, Governor Dixy's most recent eradication program was only partially successful before the environmental groups caught wind of it. Now the operation is under the jurisdiction of the Department of Wildlife and the whole boondoggle is being held up in the courts due to injunctions filed by several of the tree-hugger outfits and whatnot.

"But you've also got to remember that it's a damned difficult . . . I'd say impossible . . . prospect to locate every single Sasquatch out there under our current silvicultural regime, especially in our roadless tracts such as the

Dark Divide. I mean, think about it. We're talking about an exceptionally intelligent creature that's perfectly adapted to its habitat. They've been here for thousands and thousands of years, longer than humans by a long shot. They know just exactly where they're safe and they're learning how to exploit our communities. That's the real issue. I mostly worry about their spring raiding parties. We lost a few good citizens and plenty of livestock the year before last. Of course, you'll never read about any of this in the traditional press, not with the state paying everybody to stay hush hush about it. I mean, can you imagine the fallout if my investigative work was brought to the light of day. It would be a bona fide firestorm. A sensation. The only reason I'm still alive and talking to you right now is because too many people would know I'd been right all along if I went missing.

"Now. What can we do about these Sasquatches? That's a good question. In my opinion they're a hazard to our rural communities on a level much higher than grizzlies or cougar. What I think we oughta do is I think we oughta log off all the forest from here to Yakima, from the Columbia on up past Mount Rainier. It would be a boon to the local economy and it would clear the Sasquatches out. I think we oughta drive them up into Canada and let the Canucks figure out what to do with them."

Shef was dumbstruck.

"Show him your books," Wilson said.

Ferlin turned and unlocked his rear window, and it creaked open to reveal a cache of at least a hundred books stacked in cardboard boxes. There were a handful of different volumes, each of them bearing a picture of the reputed creature in various menacing poses. Titles like *Hairy Devils* and *Surviving Sasquatch*. Ferlin reached down and grabbed a book.

"Would you like it autographed?" he asked Shef.

"A signed copy is a true collector's item," Wilson said in a convincing tone.

Shef shrugged. "Sure. Thanks."

Ferlin scrawled his name on the title page and passed the book to the rookie. "Here you go, son."

Shef received the comically thin book and asked, "Who's your publisher?"

"At this point I'm still doing it all myself. And I'll keep on that way if I've got to. The whole enterprise has been a money pit, but it's worth it if it saves even one person's life."

"How many Sasquatches have you seen personally?" Shef asked sarcastically.

"Only one," Ferlin said. He faced Shef with a grave expression. "One was enough."

There was a dramatic pause as Ferlin recalled what appeared to be a haunting memory. He looked powerfully affected, and he took a long deep breath and blew it out shaking his head.

"So, what should I do if I find a Sasquatch when I'm on patrol? Can I shoot it?"

"Not unless you want the environmental groups on your ass for the rest of your natural born life. But if you do shoot one you're a hero in my eyes, and you'd better call me up just as quick as you can. I've still got a reward going for any Sasquatch pelt. Male, female, juvenile. It doesn't matter which."

Wilson finally interrupted. "Well, Ferlin. I think we'd better get back on patrol. Appreciate you taking the time to educate the rookie."

"It's my honor."

"And Shef, why don't you fish around in your pocket there and pass Ferlin a ten. His cause runs on donations."

"Ten dollars?" Shef said.

"Ah, I didn't mean for him to have to pay me," Ferlin said. "But heck. Any amount helps fund my ongoing research."

Shef grudgingly counted out five ones and a five and held out the money. Ferlin took it with great cheer and humility.

"It's going to be a pleasure having you in this district. And I hope you enjoy the book. Well, gentlemen. I'll see you around."

The deputies got back in the squad car and Wilson pulled out and headed north. Shef was flipping through the poorly photographed chap-book, its pages uncentered and bound by staples.

"I can't believe you made me pay ten dollars for this crap."

"Trust me. It was money well spent."

"You've actually read all those books?"

"I haven't read any of them."

"But you believe all this stuff about Bigfoot?"

"Of course I don't."

Shef spun around and waved his hands up in the air. "Then why the hell did you make me buy the book?"

"Because Ferlin Blackstone is the best informant Clark County has ever had. And your ten-dollar donation just made him your newest best friend. Ferlin goes everywhere. He sees everything. I can't tell you how many drug operations he's helped us bust. All these guys growing dope and brewing PCP do it way out in the woods where he's hiking around looking for Sasquatches. And he finds them for us. The drugs, I mean."

"Really? That wacko is a top informant."

"Don't judge a book by its cover, Shef. Except that one in your hands. That one there is a jumbled-up mess of garbage."

T he past days had brought the worst snowstorm in thirty years, and now that it was melting the weathermen were calling for floods. Wilson was working late into the evening again, a week of long hours assisting public utility crews and stranded motorists. He was making his final round of the district when dispatch notified him of a bar fight at Doug's Tavern.

Wilson doubled back toward town and entered Yacolt. The tavern was ahead on his right and Wilson drove past it slowly, made a U-turn, and cruised by it once more. Several windows were broken and glass shards and beer mugs littered the sidewalk. He parked his squad car out front and went on to the tavern door as a drunk man bleeding from his nose attempted to weave past. Wilson grabbed the drunk by the shoulder and herded him back inside.

"Take a seat," Wilson directed.

The man wiped his nose on his sleeve like a sullen child and sat at one of the only upright tables. Next to him stood another barfly whose shirt had been ripped to tatters and hung from him like some flag of a lost cause. He too sat.

With the scene contained Wilson took a moment to survey the tavern and found it imbued with a queer calm considering the utter wreckage of broken stools and shattered glass and the reek of cheap spilled beer. Perhaps a dozen patrons were accentuating postures of meek innocence, registering Wilson's presence and continuing to gaze at nothing in particular. Wilson turned his attention to a young redhead with an imbecilic gape-mouthed expression and a purple knot swelling from his forehead.

"Mind explaining what happened here?" Wilson asked.

Through bloodshot eyes and the fogged look of a concussion the man gazed at Wilson and then pinned his eyes to the calendar on the wall.

"You need me to call you an ambulance?" Wilson asked.

He shook his head no.

"Where's the bartender?"

He shrugged.

Wilson took a step toward the next man, a timid old sot who seemed to deflate in his chair. "I know you. You work at the hardware store. Tell me what happened."

He began fidgeting with his hands.

"Go on," Wilson said. "Start explaining."

The old sot tried to sneak a furtive glance over his shoulder, searching for direction it seemed from three men lounging astride the bar. He looked back at Wilson. "I'm not saying."

Wilson made his way over to the trio along the bar. Two of them were grinning like schoolyard bullies, and the largest of the three was smoking a cigarette and leaning back with a cool look of insouciance.

Wilson stopped just out of arm's reach with his hands on his hips. "Griswold Frye," he said. "Welcome home."

Griz didn't seem to register Wilson at all. Very casually he lifted his shot, swallowed half the contents, and then stared at the glass as if he were ruminating on what all was left.

"I said, welcome home, Griz."

"I heard you," he said with a raspy drawl.

"Why don't you tell me how this place got all torn up?"

Griz looked around like he was just seeing the place for the first time. Finally, he looked at Wilson, his eyes nearly crossed and oddly sensitive. Like a lure. "Just been here enjoying my whiskey. Got no information for you."

"For some reason, I find that hard to believe."

Griz remained absolutely motionless and one of the others took up the topic, a sneering scofflaw with a shaved head.

"We had nothing to do with this," he said placing his hand over his heart. "Scout's honor, officer. Officer . . . Wilson. If you don't believe us then just ask these other guys. Maybe they can straighten it all out for you."

"They don't seem interested in talking."

"They don't? Well, shucks. I guess you're just out of luck then."

"You think you might know more if we asked you some questions back at the station?"

"Go on and take me." He held his wrists out. "But I'm not gonna be too helpful."

Wilson folded his arms over his chest. "I see. Tell me, where is the bartender?"

"She's back in the back somewhere. Said something about a mop and a bucket. You want me to call her for you? Darlene. Oh Darlene, dear."

In a moment the mousy little bartender appeared with a broom and dust pan in one hand while using the handle of a mop to steer its bucket through the melee. She wore glasses and looked like she'd had better days. She gave Wilson a weary look.

"How are you, Darlene?"

"I'm fine," she seethed, her eyes darting between Wilson and Griz.

Wilson gestured to the tavern at large. "So, what would you like me to do?"

"I wasn't the one that called you. I've got it under control."

"Doug's not gonna be happy about this. He's gonna want to know who started it."

"It's a tavern. Fights happen."

"He might not feel the same way."

"Then it's between him and me. Like I said, I've got it under control."

Wilson turned around and addressed the entire patronage. "Anybody wants to get something off their chest, now's the time."

He waited for someone to speak. The scofflaw began snickering quietly. Finally, the drunk with the bloody nose stood and announced he was leaving. Wilson let him go and soon the others were filing out behind him. Only the three at the bar remained. They ordered another round and Wilson stood there staring at Griz until he finally made eye contact.

"What?" Griz said.

"You'll be back in the slammer in under a month you keep this shit up."

"You don't know me."

"Not yet I don't. But I'm looking right at you and I can tell you're no good."

"Hey," the scofflaw interrupted. "You can't—"

"Shut the fuck up," Wilson told him and the scofflaw sulked back into his seat. Wilson let his hand rest on the holster of his gun as he leaned in close to Griz. "I'd like you to know that I take pride in cleaning garbage like you off my streets."

Griz smiled. "You're awfully brave without a backup."

"And you're awfully stupid for an ex-con."

They stared at each other for a long fraught moment, and then Griz swallowed the rest of his shot and pulled a wad of cash from his pocket. He set a few bills on the counter and stood. "Let's roll, boys. Barney Fife here ain't gonna let us drink in no peace."

Scowling, the other two followed suit. While they were exiting, one of them made a crude joke about Wilson's mother, and they were all cackling as the door swung shut behind them.

In the corner of the room the bartender was sweeping glass shards into a pile. She seemed determined to ignore Wilson. He walked over and offered her his help, but she waved him away.

"Don't even bother asking me about it because I've got nothing to say," she said as she took up the dustpan.

"They're not allowed to intimidate you like this."

She huffed and swept up a clinking pile of glass.

"You're better off if you let me help you."

She paused mid-sweep and fixed him a sympathetic look. "If you really want to help, then go drag Doug's drunk ass down here. Otherwise, leave me alone. You don't know what it's like living out here with these maniacs."

"That's why we've got to put them away."

"You do what you think is right. But you leave me out of it."

L ate the next morning Wilson returned to the tavern. He parked and stepped out into the street that glistened with snowmelt under the bright sun and the cerulean sky. Citizens paced the sidewalks with newfound purpose now that the thaw was on. Wilson greeted a few elderly ladies and then walked up and banged on the tavern door.

From within there came a shout that the tavern was closed. As Wilson banged the door again he heard faint cursing and the aggressive unlatching of bolts. Doug swung open the door.

"Oh, it's you," he said.

"Can I come in?"

Doug let him pass. He was unshaven and his eyes had the glaze of an enduring hangover. He looked over the rubble of demolished bar furnishings and then flapped his arms like a pathetic flightless bird. "So, who the hell did this to me?"

"Darlene wouldn't talk to you either?"

"She wouldn't give me any names. She even tried to give me some lip about how this is just the risk of owning a tavern."

"I wouldn't be too hard on her. She's scared of them."

"Scared of who, goddamnit?"

"A few new thugs. I think they're trying to overrun the local drug scene. Might be what the fight was all about. The only one I recognized goes by the name of Griz. I'll try and bring you a few mugshots of him."

"So why didn't you take him out of here in handcuffs?"

"Because nobody would talk. There's not a lot I can do when even the bartender won't cooperate with me."

"Yeah, well, she doesn't work for me anymore."

Doug stooped down and rocked a battered dining table on its side, only one of its legs still attached. He let it fall to the ground and then toed through a scatter of wonky chairs.

"How much damage did they do?" Wilson asked.

"More than I can afford."

"Insurance gonna cover it?"

"I haven't been keeping up with the payments."

"You can get into trouble like that."

"I'm already in trouble. The bar hasn't been making any money. The finances are . . . well, they're fucked. And I can't seem to get 'em straight. I think maybe somebody's been stealing from me."

Doug went and laid his forehead against the wooden bartop etched with initials and the filthy mottos of idle liquored minds. He moaned and rolled his head back and forth. When he straightened up again his forehead bore the imprint of three backward K's.

"I'm screwed, Tom. I mean, I'm tapped out. Broke. And now Bethany's trying to come after me for back child support. The other day she told me she won't let me see my boy until I start coming up with some money."

There was the sound of laughter and Wilson looked through one of several broken windows, a few pedestrians shuffling through the jagged holes made by pool balls and beer mugs.

Doug had been watching him with a sheepish look. Wilson caught it and somehow knew what was coming next.

"We're pals aren't we, Tom?"

Wilson didn't reply.

"I know we don't always see eye to eye, but I was wondering if—"

"I can't do it, Doug."

"Hear me out. It wouldn't have to be much money. In fact, you could think of it as an investment in the tavern. I could make you a partner even. On a percentage basis. I'm only talking about a couple grand maybe. Just enough to get me over the hump. I need some help."

It was the hope in his eyes that Wilson found saddest of all. That he could even consider such a possibility. "I think you oughta talk to your Pops about it."

Doug shook his head. "He cut me off."

"Then I don't know what to say. I can't be investing in a tavern. I'm saving up for another baby."

Doug sat there stoically like one receiving a guilty verdict and then leaned over the bar and rummaged with the bottles. He returned with a fifth of rum and he unscrewed the cap and took a long swig, nearly gagging at the end of it.

"Seriously, dude? It's not even noon."

"Just leave me alone with my shitty life."

"Have you talked to the bank yet?"

"I said, leave me alone!" he shouted almost desperately.

"Take it easy, Doug. Why don't we . . ."

Doug's chin had fallen to his chest. Wilson nearly put his hand on his shoulder, but he couldn't quite bring himself to do it. After a long time, Doug finally raised his head, his eyes red and glassy. When he spoke, his voice sounded hoarse, distant.

"I thought things would be different for me here. I thought if I moved back near the family that maybe I could be a better kind of person. But I'm just the same failure as always. God . . . I'm so sick of being me."

Wilson shifted his stance, uneasy, uncertain what to say. Outside on the street a log truck was passing through town with its enormous engine rumbling like a war machine and they turned and watched it pass there and there through the succession of broken windows.

When the sound of the truck had all but vanished Wilson asked, "You eaten yet today?"

Doug shook his head no.

"Come on then. Let's get some grub. I haven't met a man yet that didn't feel better after a big plate of biscuits and gravy."

Doug sighed and stood and replaced the rum behind the bar. He swung into his leather jacket and they headed for the door.

"You mind if we go to Chelatchie?" Doug asked.

"What's wrong with Dolores' place?"

Doug finally cracked a subdued grin. "Ah, you know. There's a waitress there that might not be too happy to see me."

Wilson held the door for him and then gave him a light kick in the pants as he passed. "It's your pecker that's your problem."

"I'm weak, Tom."

"You're a whore is what you are."

Near the end of his shift, Wilson pulled up to the Vertner residence. He parked and ambled up the driveway where Virgil lay underneath his decrepit Ford truck still stranded on blocks. He was cranking on a wrench and seemed to be deriving his power from an artful slew of profanities.

"Need any help there?" Wilson asked.

The unexpected voice made Virgil flinch and then holler out in pain. "Sonofabitch. That took some skin off the old knuckles."

"Sorry to startle you there."

"That's alright. I am bleeding though."

Virgil reached out for a grease-soaked rag, wrapped his skinned knuckles with it, and then slid out from under the truck. He stood and adjusted his glasses. "You want me to fetch him for you?"

"No. I think he saw me already."

"Really appreciate you helping us out like this."

"It's no problem. I'm glad to do it."

"You'll let me pay you back now, won't you?"

"Don't worry about it."

"Nah. You let me pay you back when I'm on my feet again."

"Well. How about you just save me some firewood this fall?"

"That's a deal. I can do that."

They both turned to watch Rodney come walking through the yard. He had on his one decent shirt and seemed to have made some effort to comb his hair.

"Look at you all slick and spiffy," Virgil said. "What do you think, he's taking you out for dinner and a movie?"

"Shut up," Rodney said as he looked around self-consciously.

"Now you mind whatever Deputy Wilson says, you hear?"

"I know."

"And remember. If Deputy Wilson gets into a real dramatic police situation out there, you might just have to walk your butt back home."

"I know. You already told me."

"Well, alright then." Virgil turned and took Wilson's hand. "Thanks again, Tom. You're a real standup guy, you know."

Rodney climbed into the passenger seat, and Wilson drove on toward the town of Battle Ground. It was the first time the boy had ever been inside a police car, and he was looking all around with fascination.

"What is that thing?" Rodney asked.

"My radar gun."

"And that?"

"Pepper spray."

"Do you wear a bulletproof vest?"

"No."

"Why not?"

"Too heavy and too expensive."

"Have you ever been shot at?"

"Yeah."

"Cool. Was he like a bank robber or something?"

"He was my uncle. We were hunting."

"That doesn't count then."

"You'd count it if you'd been there with me."

"But that's not what I meant. I meant, have you been shot at while you were working."

"Then no. Not yet."

"But someday you probably will get shot at, right?"

He took his time to weigh the odds and said, "Maybe."

"Then you should wear a bulletproof vest. It could save your life."

Wilson chuckled at the boy's innocent charm, and they rolled on as Rodney began to examine the radar gun and fiddle with its controls. In town, Wilson made a few sweeping turns and pulled into the DMV parking lot. They were heading for the entrance when Ferlin Blackstone swung through the door, the hulking Sasquatch hunter spotting Wilson and grabbing ahold of his shoulder.

"You are just the man I wanted to see. Boy, have I got something for you."

"What's up, Ferlin?"

"Maybe you should steady yourself first."

"You've got me covered in that department already. What's up?"

"Mount St. Helens is awakening from her slumber."

"Awakening? How do you figure that?"

"Cause there's been all kinds of chatter on the Forest Service radio frequency about it."

"They're saying the mountain's going to erupt?"

"They're saying there's been an earthquake."

"Where?"

"They're saying the epicenter was eighteen miles northeast of the mountain, but what I think—"

Wilson moved toward the door. "I'm sorry, Ferlin, but I've really got to get Rodney some new tabs before this place closes up."

"Just hold your horses for two minutes. The official story is that some seismographs picked up a four-point-one magnitude quake with an epicenter eighteen miles northeast of the mountain. But I think there's been a mistake. I think some dufus misinterpreted the data. It doesn't make any sense that the epicenter would be located way out there."

"So, based on what you overheard on the radio you think all the experts have got it wrong about this earthquake?"

"That's what I'm saying."

"And you think that this one minor earthquake means that the mountain is becoming active?"

"I sense your skepticism. That's healthy. But you should know that she's overdue for an eruption. Go ahead and look it up. I think things are about to get very exciting around here."

"Huh. Well, that's a pretty interesting theory you've got there. I guess we'll just see what they say about it in the paper tomorrow."

"Can't always trust those papers, Tom. You know that. I'm just saying, I'd be getting ready for an eventful spring if I were you."

When Wilson was finally able to escape from Ferlin's outlandish theories, he and Rodney went inside and took a number and found a pair of seats.

"What if what he says is true?" Rodney asked. "What if the mountain really is waking up?"

"Don't worry about what he was saying. Ferlin's a nice guy, but he's a wingnut. I'm a lot more likely to trust whoever's interpreting those seismographs than someone who believes that Bigfoot is a menace to society."

"What's Bigfoot been doing?"

"What? No. It's nonsense. Just like this talk about the mountain probably is."

"But what if he's right? That would be really scary. That would be like—"

"Hey. What number did I give you?"

Rodney looked at the ticket. "Seventy-three."

"They just called seventy-one so let's be ready. You got your driver's license handy?"

"It's right here."

"Good."

A camera flashed in the corner and the young woman being photographed began pleading to have another picture taken.

"Deputy Wilson?" the boy asked.

"Yeah."

"How come you're helping me out like this?"

"Because I can."

"But why me?"

"Because I like you."

"Most people don't like me."

"That's not true."

"Yeah it is. Most people think I'm a loser."

"Well. Most people are wrong about a lot of things."

I t had been days since the tremors began and the citizenry could barely tolerate another subject. That afternoon more than a dozen locals were congregated at the Fargher Lake General Store, and the crowded little establishment resounded with their boisterous speculations. After more than a century their comely backyard volcano seemed to be awakening and everyone wanted to have a say.

Wilson stood in the corner of the store sipping a cup of coffee and gazing through the window. Somewhere out there beyond the farmhouses and the blueberry fields of that agrarian community, somewhere lost to the gray haze of that dismal spring, somewhere far too close for comfort, the mountain was trembling. Quaking down in her magmatic deeps. Wilson was meditating on what it might mean for him when a man smacked him on the arm.

"What do you think, deputy?" asked a porcine timberman.

Wilson turned. "What do I think about what?"

"Mount St. Helens. Is she just burping or is she gonna blow her top?"

The group of citizens were waiting to see how he would respond. He picked his words carefully, fear a contagion at that moment.

"The scientists don't seem overly concerned about it. I think it's best to just take it a day at a time for now."

"Well, I think she's gonna blow for sure," said the timberman. "And we've got front row seats. This here is a once in a lifetime experience."

"I'm scared of it," said a nervous housewife.

"Ain't nothing to be scared of," said the timberman. "All that sucker's gonna do is spew some lava for us and then quiet back down again."

"How do you know? You a geologist?"

"You work in the woods long enough, you get a good feel for these things."

"Ah, you're full of pooey," said the woman.

"Fine then. Let's bet on it."

"I don't gamble. Gambling's a sin."

"No it ain't."

"Yeah it is."

"Ain't no sin."

A lanky farmer in overalls hooked his thumbs underneath his shoulder straps and directed himself toward Wilson. "Let's say the mountain does blow. You guys working for the county got any sort of emergency plan in place?"

"We're working on that," Wilson said.

"Cause I got me a hayfield and a herd of cattle and I'd like to know what I'm supposed to do with them if we get any kind of an ash fallout."

"You're worried about your cows?" said the woman. "What about your family? What about my children? What if the mountain blows while they're at school? First we got to worry about the Soviets bombing us. Now this. I don't like it. I don't think it's exciting."

Wilson took a step forward. "A lot of people are nervous, Tina. As they have a right to be. But as of now the scientists are saying an eruption is unlikely, so let's all stay calm and keep our heads screwed on tight."

"It's gonna blow for sure," said the timberman.

"Would you stop that already," said the woman.

Wilson headed for the door. "You all need anything, you just give me a call."

All afternoon he listened to the news on the radio, cruising through the district and bending to hear any update on the mountain. It was going on dusk when he received a report of shoplifting and he drove on for the Amboy Market.

The supervisor was standing outside the entrance when he arrived, a rigid young man with lacquered hair and a tie and a name tag clipped to his breast pocket. He reached out and shook Wilson's hand with undue vigor. "Thanks for getting here so quickly."

"Just doing my job."

"Well, we've got her back in the office for you. Martin's been watching over her."

"Alright. Let's go see what she has to say."

The supervisor led Wilson into the grocery and down a narrow aisle filled with ladies scrutinizing labels.

"What all did she try to make off with?" Wilson asked.

"A whole basket of stuff. Some soups, some pasta. A gallon of milk."

"She try to run on you?"

"Oh no. Just tried walking out as casual as could be."

They passed the deli and went through a pair of swinging doors and came to the office. The supervisor knocked and they stepped inside. A man in a checker's uniform greeted them. Behind him sat Louanne.

"Tom," she shouted. "Thank heavens it's you."

"Louanne? What's going on here?"

"These two men have been holding me captive."

"They're saying you tried to shoplift from their store."

"That's what they keep saying, but it doesn't make a lick of sense. These two are a couple of goons if you ask me. Holding me against my will like this."

"You were trying to steal from us," said the supervisor.

"I was not stealing. I've never stolen a thing in my life."

"Well, you were certainly trying to today."

Wilson stepped forward and put his hand in the air for silence. "Louanne, what happened to your receipt?"

"Well, that's the funny part about it."

"She kept telling us she must have lost it," said the supervisor. "But we asked all of the checkers and each of them swore they never rung her up. We searched all over the store and couldn't find a stray receipt."

"She must have eaten it," joked the checker.

Wilson turned and pointed at him. "You. Dumbass. Get up and get out of this room."

"What?"

"Now."

The checker glared at Wilson but stood and left without a word.

"She doesn't have any money either," continued the supervisor. "No cash, no checkbook. Not even a credit card on her."

"I don't understand it," Louanne said, her voice breaking. "It couldn't have happened the way they're saying. I'm not a thief."

"I know that," Wilson said. "We're gonna get this all straightened out, okay. Just hang tight here in the office for two minutes while he and I have a quick chat. Then we'll be on our way."

Wilson and the supervisor stepped outside the office.

"You must not know who she is," Wilson said.

The supervisor looked at the door and shook his head.

"That's Sheriff Jenkins' wife."

"Crap."

"And she's starting to come down with Alzheimer's. You know what that is don't you?"

"Like dementia."

"That's right. So despite what she might say, she probably doesn't have the foggiest clue what happened earlier. If anything like this happens again I want you to call me or Sheriff Jenkins directly. I'm writing his number down on the back of my card. What I don't want you to ever do again is to keep her locked up in your office like this. You got it? Now here's some money for the groceries she wanted. Go on and ring me up if you wouldn't mind."

The supervisor took the money. "I'm awful sorry about this."

"So am I."

Wilson followed Louanne home, and he unloaded the groceries from her trunk and carried them inside for her. In the kitchen, he set the bags down on the counter and she began putting things away in the cupboards.

"Where did Les get off to today?" Wilson asked.

"I don't know. He usually does whatever he wants."

"He say what time he'd be back?"

"Suppertime, I'd imagine. He's not one to miss a meal."

"In that case, I think I'll wait here for him if that's alright with you."

"You know you're always welcome. Would you like a cup of coffee while you wait?"

"That'd be nice."

Wilson watched her open the refrigerator, pause for a moment, and then place the gallon of milk behind another jug that had yet to be opened. He quickly looked away and took up a newspaper from the dining table that was dated from the previous month and bore the front-page headline *Boy beats FBI to Cooper loot.*

"You must be keeping this one as a souvenir," Wilson said.

"Oh yeah. We're having a special frame made for that issue."

"Les must have been excited."

"That's putting it mildly. He was howling like he'd been quilled by a porcupine." Wilson chuckled as Louanne put some water on to boil. "I ever tell you about how hard we looked for that rascal?"

She had, but Wilson asked to hear it again. Louanne set some cream and sugar on the table and then took a seat.

"Well, that was in seventy-one," she said. "Les was still sheriff then, of course, so when the FBI told him that D.B. Cooper had probably landed in this area he offered to help them search for him and the money. Funniest thing about it was that the first place they had Les search was in our own backyard. Said it was right in the flight path. Then they had him going door to door checking our neighbors' barns and sheds and all sorts of places. It was really something."

"Not too often you get to hunt down an airplane hijacker. Must have been a thrill."

"It was. Only wish we could have found him."

"What do you think happened to him?"

"Well, I'll tell you. And Les and I aren't the only ones who think this. He probably turned into fish food at the bottom of Lake Merwin. Probably got his parachute hung up on a snag and couldn't bust loose. That's what I think. Probably down there at the bottom of Lake Merwin just like my old house the government flooded when they built the dam. He might've even got hung up on one of my family's locust trees. Wouldn't that be a kick in the pants?"

The kettle on the stove was whistling and Louanne took it off and poured the water over some scoops of instant coffee and set a mug in front of Wilson. Then she poured another cup for herself and sat again.

"Can I tell you a little secret?" she said.

He nodded.

"You can't tell Les."

"I give you my word," Wilson said as he raised his palm.

"I would have kept some of that ransom money if I had ever found it."

"But weren't the bills marked?"

"Golly. I wouldn't have spent it. I just would have kept a few bills as a keepsake."

Wilson smiled and stirred his coffee. "Yeah, I might have done the same."

Louanne swiveled around in her chair. "Pardon me for just a moment. I need to use the ladies room."

She padded down the hall and into the bathroom. Wilson drank his coffee and was skimming through the newspaper article when the phone on the wall began ringing.

"Tom, would you answer that for me," Louanne hollered.

Wilson rose and lifted the receiver. "Hello."

"You might be retired, but you're still a pig." The voice was spooky and unnatural, purposely distorted.

"Who is this?"

"I'm the big bad wolf. And I might come blow your house down."

"Listen up, you——"

The line went dead. Wilson stood there listening to the empty tone until he heard the toilet flush. He hung the phone back up and in a moment Louanne returned.

"Who was that on the phone?" she asked.

He gazed at her cheerful wrinkled face, so kind and curious despite slipping into senility.

"Telemarketer," he said.

She shook her head. "They just never give up, do they?"

W ilson had the day off and he sat in the passenger seat of the old Chevy as the sheriff drove them up Spirit Lake Highway. The ordinarily tranquil road was now choked with traffic, and at Silver Lake it seemed like nothing less than a carnival.

Hundreds of spectators lined the highway and all eyes were on the distant mountain, which was right then sending a billowing white cloud of steam belching some thousand feet into the air. Intrepid tourists stood spellbound. Children were pointing and screeching and putting binoculars back to their eyes. Old folks lounged in lawn chairs and sipped from thermoses while young men walked around hawking any gimmicky trinket they'd found time to slap a half-clever pun upon.

Wilson rolled his window down, and as they progressed, several separate melodies drifted from this stereo and that while he called out for the sheriff the more remote license plates from as far away as Texas and New York and Wisconsin. Overhead, more than twenty small airplanes were buzzing around in a steady circle, their pilots awaiting clearance to approach the mountain.

"Boy, this is some kind of spectacle, ain't it?" said the sheriff.

"I've never seen anything like it," Wilson agreed.

Up ahead, a long line of sightseers waited outside a mobile home some entrepreneur had converted into a barbecue joint. As they passed, a rich, porky smoke wafted by and made their mouths water.

"I always hoped I'd live long enough to see her blow," said the sheriff. "Looks like I just squeaked it in."

They stopped to let a camper van parallel park, and as they were waiting a zealous youth thrust a t-shirt up to the passenger window.

"Only five dollars," the boy announced.

"What's it say?" asked the sheriff.

"Says, *Mount St. Helens, lava or leave it.*"

"I'll take two."

"Right on. What sizes would you like? I'm all out of extra-large."

"One small and one large."

"Coming right up," said the boy as he dug through his backpack.

"Would you like one, Tommy?"

"No need. Ellen already got me one just like it."

The boy passed Wilson the t-shirts and they continued up the highway. Ten miles below Spirit Lake they arrived at another congestion of vehicles and then the roadblock. A pair of weary-eyed Cowlitz County deputies stood before a sandwich-board sign declaring that the highway ahead was closed. One of the deputies began motioning for the sheriff to turn around and head back down the road, but the sheriff only inched his truck closer to the barricade. The deputy shook his head with impatience, strolled over, and leaned in with his hand against the driver's side door.

"Can't let you fellas get any closer. Governor's orders."

"I own a cabin on Spirit Lake," said the sheriff. "I'd like to clear out my valuables in case we get a big eruption."

"In that case, I'm going to need to see some proof of ownership."

"They're all back at the house."

"Then I'm sorry, but I can't let you through."

"You're telling me I've got to drive all the way home and back and show you my papers just to access my own property?"

"I'm sorry, sir. Orders are we've got to see something proving your ownership of the property before we can let you through."

"This is the United States of America, correct?"

The deputy took his hand from the sheriff's truck, stepped back, and folded his arms across his chest. "Sir. If we let every knucklehead through that wanted to get close to that mountain, we'd have about a thousand citizens out there endangering their lives. Besides that, it's the governor's orders. Take it up with her if you're upset."

"Well, this is just asinine," said the sheriff.

"Move it along," commanded the deputy.

Wilson finally leaned in to the conversation. "Hello," he said, waving at the deputy. "Let's try this again. I'm Tom Wilson, Clark County Deputy. And this is Lesley Jenkins, our former sheriff. Here's my badge. Mind if we get through?"

The deputy shifted his stance and his face softened into a smile. "Hell, fellas. That's all you had to say."

The last stretch of highway meandered east along the Toutle River which sparkled turquoise in the brilliant midday sun. They were each watching for the mountain, but it was mostly concealed behind a green wall of hemlock, fir, and bigleaf maples. Weyerhaeuser trucks roared by intermittently hauling loads of mammoth old-growth trees, and they began to pass clearcuts with signs along the highway reading *Your Forest 2025.*

"What do you say we go drop in on Harry before we hit the cabin," the sheriff said as he turned off for Spirit Lake. "I'm curious to see how he's been handling all this craziness."

"You mean, Harry Truman?"

"Of course."

"You guys are friends?"

"Something like that."

They passed a sign for Mount St. Helens Lodge and began down the drive in a few inches of lingering snow. They were but fifty yards from the front door when the sheriff stopped and had a chuckle.

"I'll be damned if he isn't holding court for all them."

Truman stood on the porch of his home half-encircled by a flock of reporters and photographers. The leathery octogenarian had his chest puffed out and was gesturing emphatically with a glass of bourbon, his life now a legend for refusing to leave the lodge that huddled in the shadow of the volcano.

"Looks like Truman's becoming a real-life folk hero," Wilson said.

"That cantankerous son of a bitch was his own hero before we elected the president that shared his name. And you know what? I'd be lying if I said he hadn't been a bit of a hero to me too back when I was a younger man. That old cuss was an absolute pioneer. God, the stories he would tell."

"Were they true?"

"Enough of them were." The sheriff had himself another mirthful laugh and then began backing up the drive. "I guess we'll just have to try him again later."

The sheriff's cabin was a two-story A-frame built of cedar and surrounded by a weathered deck and a lawn that blossomed with wildflowers in the summer months. At the bottom of the property a wooden dock stretched out into the lake and supported a three-man canoe upside down against the elements. Beyond this Spirit Lake was still mostly iced over and stained from the ash that had sifted down from the volcano towering but a few scant miles from the southern shore.

Wilson and the sheriff stood near the lake's edge and watched another small eruption spewing from the volcano's charred crater, the plume expanding and churning and then thinning to wisps as the ash again dusted the mountain's flanks and the woods below.

"It's beautiful," said the sheriff.

He seemed locked in reverie as the earth began to faintly quiver, a dull rumble emanating from some unaccountable source. They shared a look.

"I could think of some other adjectives for it," said Wilson.

"Yeah, we'd better get on with it."

A few hours later the sun had set on their endeavors, and the sheriff finally decided to call it quits. The bed of his Chevy was stacked with boxes and appliances and the less cumbersome furniture. Both of them had worked up a light sweat, and the sheriff went and retrieved a six-pack of beer from where he'd left it chilling in the lake.

He cracked open two of the bottles and passed one to Wilson and they sat side by side on the porch sipping the beer in the crisp purple dusk. In the distance the mountain was but a dim outline that was being erased further by the closure of night, and a vague puff of vapor hung over the peak where several planes still buzzed around like mosquitoes, their strobes winking red in that faraway.

Wilson sat ruminating on the disturbing phone call that had been meant for the sheriff. All day it had been in his thoughts but he still figured telling about it wouldn't do anything but distress the sheriff's already troubled mind.

"What can you tell me about a guy named Griswold Frye?" Wilson finally asked.

The sheriff turned to him quickly with a look of great interest. "Why you asking?"

"Because he's back out on the streets and already causing trouble. Sergeant Davies said you used to know him pretty well."

The sheriff seemed to be studying some collection of dusty memories. "Griz," he said.

"Yeah. He and some pals tore up your grandson's tavern pretty good. He didn't tell you about that?"

"Douglas and I haven't been on the best of terms lately."

"I'm sorry to hear that."

"It's alright. We'll work it out." He took a drink of his beer. "I've known Griswold since he was about four years old. He grew up in a filthy little cabin out by Buncombe Hollow and he had things pretty rough as a youngster. His parents were both drunks and neglected him something awful. His whole family was a mess. At one time or another I jailed his dad, two of his uncles, his brother, and even his mom for a drunk and disorderly. Thank God most of them moved on or quieted down.

"Anyways, Griswold turned out about like you'd expect. By the time he was thirteen I started picking him up for this and that and sending him off to juvie. Didn't do nothing but make him meaner. Finally, I nabbed him for stealing some kid's bicycle and I asked him, is this really what you want to be doing with the rest of your life? Getting shipped off to some detention center? And he said no. So I said, if it's money that you're after then I've got some work for you over at my place. Helping out with the cattle and fixing up the barn and this and that. He said okay. And for quite a while it worked out good. He was always a bright kid and he seemed to like the work. We even got him cutting hay for some of the neighbors. He turned out to be a pretty good little businessman, and most of all he was staying out of trouble.

"But then one day our granddaughter Julie came home after her freshman year of college and for some reason she took a liking to him. Guess she was always a bit of a hayseed herself. Well, she and Griswold started to have something of a romance, and of course her pops caught wind of it. And once he figured out what kind of a dude she was fooling around with he told her he flat forbid her to see him. I thought he was probably a bit heavy-handed about it, though I certainly understood his feelings. Doesn't take more than one roll in the hay and you've suddenly got a wild buck for a son-in-law.

"He told Julie that he wouldn't pay for anymore of her schooling unless she cut it off with him and she didn't take it well. She fought him and cussed him out and called him a tyrant, but eventually she saw the light. Well, right about then her pops had to go out of town for some business and Julie felt so wretched about the whole thing that she barely would even leave the house, so guess who had to break the news to young Griswold? I wouldn't have done it except that he kept on asking me about her. Asking and asking. Finally, I couldn't stand it anymore so I told him that Julie had quit him.

"And that was that. Didn't matter that I had nothing to do with it all, but he blamed me. And it was never anything but trouble with him from then on. He actually tried to burn my barn down. Three of our cows turned up dead. And that was just at the beginning. We crossed paths after that more than a few times, usually when I was in uniform, and it never was a pretty sight. Have to admit I was awfully relieved when I learned he was going to be locked up for so long."

Wilson drained his beer and set it on the porch and took up another. "You think he might still be bitter enough about it to come after you?"

The sheriff lit up a cigarette and took a drag. "I'd say no way, but he's one I'd never lay a wager on about anything. With him and a few others I've learned there's a certain amount of vindictiveness in this world that you've just got to get accustomed to."

Wilson was looking out at the lake.

"Tommy?" the sheriff asked.

"Yeah."

"Is there something I need to know about?"

Wilson turned to the sheriff who was watching him with a look of total stoicism hard-earned by many close encounters with death and coming out on the other end stronger for it.

"No," Wilson said. "But I'll let you know if I hear of anything and you do the same. He's my bad guy to catch now. You've got enough to worry about with Louanne."

The sheriff leaned back. "Ain't that the truth. You know what she did yesterday?"

"What?"

"She served me cat food in my cereal bowl."

Wilson stifled a laugh.

"That's alright," said the sheriff. "It was funny as hell. She caught me sniffing at it and told me I was just being picky and then took a big spoonful and started chewing it up."

Wilson let himself hoot and the sheriff began wheezing right along.

"I couldn't believe it, but she swallowed it down and went for another spoonful. Said it must have just been approaching its due date."

They went on laughing for a long time, longer and louder than either of them had in a good while, their bellows echoed by the forest and then distilled into the night.

When they'd quieted down the sheriff said, "I never knew it could happen so fast. Some days it's like she's hardly even the same person she was. She's not even gone and I already miss her. Isn't that a thing to say? I miss my wife."

Wilson let out a breath, then glanced sidelong at the sheriff and saw that he was crying. Wilson stood and walked over and put his hand on the back of the sheriff's head as the old man wept. He knew of nothing that could redeem what the sheriff was losing, could think of no true words of comfort. And so Wilson said nothing, offered but his bare hand to help ward off that dark sorrow.

Finally, the sheriff patted Wilson's arm and stood and took a manly swig of beer. With the bottle still aloft, he paused and squinted through the night at the silhouettes of two deer that had crept into the yard and were feeding cautiously. Farther out in the lake, an osprey was sounding a series of shrill calls, and yonder yet, out there in the wild beyond, the volcano's breath was like a whisper on a frigid night. Subtle proof of the deep earth's rise.

T he winds had changed and Wilson awoke to find his entire neighborhood coated in a fine layer of volcanic ash. His truck looked like it had been run through a flour mill, and he stood there in the breaking dawn wondering what he was supposed to do about it.

From the garage he grabbed a few old rags and tried wiping the ash from his windshield. His efforts were producing a grating sound he knew was wrong so he stared with puzzlement and then looked down the block to see if there was any neighbor around who might have discovered a better method. He seemed to be the only one up at that hour so he walked around to the yard and returned with a bucket of hose water. With one adroit heave, he sloshed the water across the windshield, and the ash congealed and slid to the hood like pancake batter. Next, he went for the hose itself, and once he'd sprayed away the ash he saw that he had in fact scratched the windshield. He looked toward the mountain, shook his head, and got in and drove to work.

At the station, the briefing room was twice as crowded as usual, every deputy working overtime since the mountain had begun stirring. Wilson spotted Shef standing next to the coffee machine and he went over and fixed himself a cup.

"How's it going, rook?" Wilson asked.

"Can't complain," Shef said. "Though they never did teach me anything in the academy about how to deal with an erupting volcano."

"Yeah, it's not generally on the syllabus."

"You hear I got bit by some kid's pet ferret?"

"Yeah. Sergeant told me."

"Had to get a rabies shot."

"Yikes."

"I'm liking the job though. Getting to know the district pretty well. The other day I met these—"

A massive hand had fallen onto his shoulder and Shef turned and saw the giant looming above and grinning.

"You look like you've got something good for us," said Wilson.

"Oh, it's the best," said the giant.

"You better tell it right this time," hollered the sergeant.

"So this guy working for a radio station in Cleveland called up the Cowlitz County Sheriff's Office and said a woman there was offering herself as a sacrifice to the volcano."

"This is a joke?" Shef asked.

"No, this happened yesterday."

"She wanted to sacrifice herself?"

"Yeah. You know, like what they used to do in all those Mexican countries down in South America. And this radio station was real serious about it. They were even offering to fly her out here if the authorities agreed to it."

"Heck, why not give it a try," Wilson said.

"So what'd they say?" Shef asked.

"One of the sergeants got on the horn and said he didn't think it would work. Said, if we're going to offer a sacrifice, we should use a . . . a . . ."

The giant was ready to laugh but he couldn't remember the word.

"A native, you dolt," hollered the sergeant.

"Yeah, that we should use a native," the giant repeated, chuckling gamely. "Man, I wish I could have been there when he said that."

"What is wrong with some of these nutjobs?" Shef asked.

Wilson smiled. "Guess they figure getting roasted alive is better than living in Cleveland."

The quip seemed to cut the giant in half and he nearly fell doubled over against the rookie.

The sergeant was observing his colossal copchild with incredulity when he overheard one of the other deputies mention the everlasting hostage crisis in Iran.

"What'd you say, Adams?" asked the sergeant.

"Crap," said the deputy.

"You know the rules."

The deputy stood with some dejection and went and folded a ten dollar bill through the slitted lid of an old Folgers coffee can.

Shef leaned in toward Wilson and said quietly, "I don't know what that's all about."

Wilson explained, "Sergeant got so sick of hearing about Iran he announced that anybody who mentions the hostage crisis while they're on the clock has to ante up ten dollars and feed it to the kitty."

"What happens with the money?"

"It stays there until somebody wins. At the end of the week we're all gonna guess the day we think the hostages will either be released or killed. Person closest to the day takes the whole pot."

Shef looked at the Folgers can. "You guys are sadistic. Can I get in on it?"

Sometime after his lunch break Wilson was cruising along a woodsy backroad only traveled by the occasional local when he came upon a yellow Corvette stopped along the shoulder. The hood was up and a sunburned man in cargo shorts and hiking boots was peering into a hissing swelter of radiator steam. The car was a Las Vegas rental, and as soiled as it was he figured it had been driven from there in a hurry.

He pulled alongside the Corvette and the petite goateed man looked up and jerked a spastic wave. In the passenger seat sat a fetching blonde woman and she beheld Wilson's presence with utter relief as he stepped out of the squad car and gave the man a polite nod.

"Would you like some help with that?"

"Pouvez-vous comprendre le français?" the man asked.

"I have no idea what you just said."

"I speak. Comment dit-on? I speak no English," he said in his faltering French accent.

"Est-ce qu'il parle espagnol?" the woman called out.

"Parlez-vous espagnol?" the man tried hopefully.

Wilson just shook his head.

"Merde," the man said.

Wilson and the Frenchman gazed upon the engine which had calmed and quieted to a sizzle. The Frenchman shrugged his shoulders.

"It's probably just overheated," said Wilson. The man looked at him blankly and Wilson tipped an imaginary jug of water above the radiator cap. "It needs coolant. Or water."

"Yes," the Frenchman said excitedly. "Water. Yes."

With that he ducked inside the Corvette and returned with a bottle of water and a towel. Then he slipped under the hood and started to twist at the radiator cap. Wilson yanked him backward and the Frenchman recovered his balance and stood glowering and also in some fear of this possibly abusive American authority.

"You have to wait for it to cool down. I know a guy who melted his face that way," Wilson said as he commenced an elaborate charade demonstrating what could happen.

The man brightened, "Bah oui. Je comprends."

They waited.

"Where are you trying to go?" Wilson asked.

The Frenchman nodded yes.

"No. Where are you going? Where? Are you going?"

"Ahh. We are from France."

"Yes, I've gathered that. But where are you going? Are you trying to visit Mount St. Helens? To see the volcano?" He made an explosion with his hands and the Frenchman became exuberant.

"*Oui. Oui.* Volcano. Yes."

Wilson finally took the towel and removed the radiator cap and topped it off with fluid. The French couple looked on like they were observing a heart valve surgery.

"Alright, that should do her," Wilson said.

He reached to shake the Frenchman's hand, but the little man drew in tight and kissed him on the cheek. Then the woman did the same. Wilson looked around in a blush.

"You folks better just follow me on to the viewpoint."

The rest of the afternoon proved tedious, and Wilson spent the end of his shift strolling through the drugstore picking up some items for his wife. A gregarious mustached woman manned the cash register and as she was tallying the goods Wilson told her the story of the wayward French visitors. When he got to where they'd kissed him, the woman tittered like a squirrel of glee and passed him his bag and receipt.

"How'd it feel getting smooched by a Frenchman?" the woman asked.

"Oh. His lips were a little chapped. And I can't recommend the goatee."

"I wish it had been me. I've always wanted to go to Paris and have me a few romances."

"Well, if those two were any representation of France then I'd just as soon rather stay home. Can't believe they would . . . Hold on, I'm getting a call."

Wilson took the radio from his hip and told the dispatcher to go ahead.

Report of shots fired at 228 Steelhead Drive. A neighbor claimed to have heard four gunshots in rapid succession. I have two units on stand-by for immediate backup.

"Can you repeat the address?" he asked.

228 Steelhead Drive. Sheriff Jenkins' place.

In but a few moments he was blazing through the nightfallen county with the emergency lights whirling red and the siren wailing like some dreadful dirge. Commuters were just returning from their jobs in the cities and Wilson was shouting for them to make way and honking and passing around blind corners. His hands had gone damp at the wheel and his throat was dry and his heart hammering like the pistons that powered his cruiser along.

To calm himself down he ran through all the benign possibilities. The sheriff was practicing with a new gun. A coyote was out in the pasture or an old cow had gone lame. It might be many things. And yet he could not drive fast enough.

Wilson skidded up the drive and saw their home lit up from within and looking pleasant as ever. He parked and drew his gun and simply stood alongside the cruiser for a moment to see what he could see. There was no activity of any kind. Only the hush of the wind in the shadowy trees.

Wilson walked up to the porch. The screen door was shut and behind it the front door mostly ajar and leaking the sound of the radio. He rang the doorbell and waited. There was no answer so he stepped inside.

"Hello," he hollered. "Hey guys, it's Tom."

He went down the hall as the radio newscaster's voice grew louder. At the stairway he took hold of the bannister and peered up toward their bedroom. The lights were all off there so he went on to the kitchen, his boot steps thudding upon the creaky wooden floor.

"Les? Louanne? Where are you guys?"

He began to sense something sinister and he cocked his pistol and held it before him. Like this he reached the cusp of the den where a small fire was dying to embers in the fireplace. The mounted bull looked down as always but otherwise the room was empty. He turned for the dining room and pushed through the parlor doors, and his eyes went straight to the picture frame on the wall for their wedding photo was now splattered with blood and hair and viscous gobs of brain. Below it the sheriff lay facedown and dead in a crimson pool of his own spilt vitality, his snowy hair streaked pink and his head looking like it had been deflated. Louanne was in the corner, on her back and still half-sitting in a fallen chair. A trickle of blood seeped from her temple and the house cat was crouched down and lapping at it.

"Oh God," Wilson said. "Not this. Please God no."

III

Statement by Sally Coombs
Eugene, Oregon
Twelve years after eruption

I'm the first to admit that being out there was totally reckless. I don't have any good excuse for it other than that we were only nineteen at the time. And Travis was always a daredevil. I adored him so much then I let him talk me into all sorts of situations my momma didn't approve of. Including getting married.

We were camped for two nights next to Coldwater Creek not all that far from Spirit Lake. That was either in the red zone or very close to it. We snuck in there one night on Travis' dual sport. I believe he had the Honda then. Or maybe it was the Yamaha. Doesn't matter.

When we got close enough to the mountain to satisfy him he hid the bike in some bushes and we made up our camp if you could call it that. We didn't even pitch a tent. He was worried that one of the planes or helicopters might spot us so we just slept under the stars. It was a real covert operation. That was how he put it. He thought he was such a renegade.

Mostly all we did was lie around and smoke grass and talk about how we were going to get rich. I guess we did catch some fish. In fact, that was the whole original purpose of the trip. Travis thought that since the area was closed off to everybody, it was going to make for the best fishing we were ever going to get. He wasn't much of a fisherman though so I think that was just his way of closing the deal to get me to go out there with him. And it was good fishing.

It was right around sunset on the second night when that man frightened us so badly. We were finishing up a game of gin rummy and it was getting pretty hard to see the cards when we heard some rustling off in the bushes. Travis thought it was a big old elk coming down for a drink of water. I was worried it might be a bear. The only thing we had to protect ourselves with was just a couple of pocket knives so we got those out and waited.

And out pops this guy. Looking all scraggly and scratched up and crazy. He seemed surprised to see us, but it didn't seem like he was afraid of us like we were of him. He really freaked me out. Right from the beginning he acted creepy. He was like, hey guys, hey there. My name's Ted. Nice to meet you. But his name wasn't Ted. Later on, I asked him what his name was again to test him and he said, I already told you. My name's Fred. But his name wasn't Fred neither. And he'd just said that his name was Ted. You see what I mean? That's very suspicious. Especially when you're way out in the woods like that.

In between all this he told us that he was heading to Spirit Lake to go meet with Harry Truman. And then he was planning on climbing up to the top of the mountain. He had an ice axe and all that kind of gear but he didn't look like a climber. And he didn't seem like he knew what he was doing either. He said he'd gotten turned around a couple times so Travis showed him on the map where we were and how to get to Spirit Lake from there.

I thought he would get going at that point since it was getting close to dark, but instead he started walking around our campsite and sort of inspecting everything with his eyes. That really upset me. I think he realized we were kind of afraid of him by that point. I think he liked it. Making us afraid.

Finally, he spotted our bag of grass and he asked if he could have some. We didn't even have time to answer before he just reached down and picked it up and took about half of it for himself. Travis was really clenching his knife by then. So was I. And just when it seemed like things might boil over he left. Barely even said a word goodbye. Just walked back into the woods.

Thankfully we never saw him again. But I did not sleep well that night. I'm not sure I even slept at all. We probably would have packed up and rode home that night except that I think Travis was a little prideful about not appearing too scared about the whole thing. But I wish we would have just gone. It was dangerous enough with the volcano ashing on us and threatening to blow. Then to think we'd had a madman in our camp. Someone who had actually killed somebody. Gosh. It still makes me a bit sick to my stomach when I think about it.

Before that I would have told you I was most afraid of the volcano or maybe the animals. But afterwards I realized that it's usually other people that you should be the most worried about.

The church was nearly full as Wilson entered with Ellen and their daughter. Perhaps two hundred people were already present to pay their respects and the afternoon sun that poured through the stained glass windows had half the congregants glowing in their grief like cinema stars.

Wilson went down the aisle and he could feel that he was being watched closely by those who knew him. Colleagues and friends curious to tell just how haunted he was by what he had seen. Wilson could look at none of them. He focused on the altar ahead, and he may have walked right up to the casket had Ellen not taken his arm and pointed out a few empty seats. They slid in next to a hunched old paper-skinned woman who turned and gave Wilson a soulful smile.

"Welcome," she said. "Thank you so much for coming."

He said a simple hello and then tried to hide his eyes.

"This sure is some kind of a turn out," she continued. "I just hope Lesley is watching it from somewhere. He'd be awfully proud to see so many people. Only I'm getting a little worried this church won't be big enough to hold everybody."

Wilson murmured something indistinguishable and the old woman began gazing at him queerly. Ellen leaned forward and took up the conversation.

"It just shows what a special man he was. How many lives he touched. I'm Ellen by the way. And these two are Tom and Maggie."

"It's very nice to meet you all," the woman said. "I'm Nancy. Louanne's big sister."

"Oh dear," Ellen said. "How is she doing?"

"Well, she's still in a coma. The doctors won't say yet if they think she'll pull through, but they've got her stable now. So that's a blessing. We're just asking for all the prayer we can get."

"We've been praying for Louanne every night. Haven't we, Maggie?"

The little girl looked up from the coloring book in her lap and nodded. Then she said, "My daddy is a policeman."

"Is he?" the old woman cooed. "Just like Lesley was, huh?"

The girl nodded again and returned to her book.

"Did you work with Lesley?" the woman asked Wilson.

His voice sounded flat and weak. "No. He was already retired before I started."

"Of course. Young as you are. So how did you folks get to know him if you don't mind me asking?"

"I work in his district."

"Oh my," she said as though she'd been stricken. "I'm sure it must have been just an absolute nightmare for whichever officer found Lesley and Louanne like that."

Wilson looked at the old woman with something close to despair and then turned away. Ellen took hold of his hand and squeezed it tightly, watching his face for some kind of a breakdown. The woman finally put it together.

"My goodness. Oh my. What a silly jabber-mouth I have."

"It's alright," Ellen said.

"Please excuse me. Both of you. I'm so sorry."

"And we're very sorry for your loss as well."

The old woman looked greatly disturbed and she began fidgeting about her seat so much her son leaned over and asked her quietly if she needed to use the restroom. She waved him off and in a moment turned and faced Wilson. Reluctantly he met her eyes.

"I know it's not right to say this in church, but I might not get to see you again," she began.

Her son tried to cut her off.

"Let me speak, Paul. I'd like him to know how I feel." The old woman's eyes had begun to smolder like hot coals. "If you catch whoever did this I hope you'll tell them that they took a great man from this world. And I also hope you'll ask them how they can justify doing what they did. I can't understand it. I can't . . ."

She had clenched her jaw to help keep her fury at bay, taking air in through her nose to calm herself down. When she was finally able to speak again her words came forth one sharply enunciated syllable at a time.

"If you're the one to catch this person, I want you to tell them not to expect any mercy from our family. You tell them that. You tell them they'd better have a long talk with God if they're interested in forgiveness. Because if it were up to me, I'd gladly see them hang. And that's what I've got to say about it."

With that the fire in her slowly extinguished and she seemed to remember again where she was. She looked up toward the rafters and said, "Pardon me, Lord, for speaking so."

When the pastor finally stepped up to the pulpit, every seat in the church was occupied and another fifty latecomers stood along the walls wherever they could fit. The pastor was a stout and serious man in wire-rimmed glasses. He had known the sheriff well and his eulogy was long and eloquent and touching. Wilson preferred to observe the audience. The policemen were easy to spot, and if they looked unengaged it was only because they'd seen so many tragedies with their own eyes. The family members were mostly in tears. Wilson noticed Doug across the room and he hung his head hugely for most of the service and lifted it but rarely.

The pastor concluded his eulogy with a call for the lawmen in attendance to continue to be brave and dutiful, to harness their grief and do battle against the evil that roams this often wicked world. Blessed are the peacemakers, he said. When the pastor was finished, he called the room to prayer.

Wilson closed his eyes and bowed his head. He was surprised to find himself communicating, but not with God. The words rolled through his head. *I will find him for you.*

When he rose up he saw that Ellen had been watching him. She looked concerned and he knew that she was scared of what would come next, how he might change, the dark intensity stored like fuel in his eyes.

"Are you okay, honey?" she asked.

He took a while to think about it. Finally, he just shook his head no.

C lear blue morning skies as Wilson drove for work, the shoulder of the interstate littered with parked cars and gawking motorists. To the northeast the mountain was ejecting a spectacular plume of ash, and as Wilson watched the display he thought that the most surreal thing about it was how ordinary the sight had become. When his eyes returned to the road ahead he saw brake lights and swerved for yet another vehicle pulling off to the shoulder. That morning he'd read in the paper that the last time the mountain was this active the eruptions had lasted for years. The new normal was just this, and it might be so for a long while to come.

At the sheriff's office he knocked on his sergeant's door and was told to come in. The detective rose to greet him, a sharp and urbane man with a falcon's nose and hair like an oil slick. They shook hands and took their seats across from the sergeant.

"How you holding up, Tom?" the sergeant asked.

"I'm okay," Wilson said.

"And how was the funeral? I was sorry I couldn't make it."

"It was good. It was . . . It was good."

The sergeant watched Wilson carefully and then nodded to the detective who tapped the yellow legal pad that rested in his lap.

"I know we already covered some of this the night of the shooting," the detective began, "but let's just go over the basics one more time to make sure we're all on the same page. You alright with that, Tom?"

"Alright."

"I appreciate it. I know this can't be easy for you."

"Part of the job, isn't it?"

"Unfortunately, that's true. Well, the first thing I wanted to tell you is that we had some of the family take a walk through the house to help us determine if anything conspicuous may have been stolen. The family's conclusion was that everything seems to be in place and that includes Louanne's purse and a whole lot of nice jewelry in plain sight in the bedroom. So obviously robbery either wasn't a prime motivator in this case or the assailant found himself in a hurry after the shooting for one reason or another.

"As far as fingerprints go we've yet to lift anything helpful and I wouldn't expect that to change. We also didn't find any unusual bootprints or tire tracks to help us. There was no sign of any bodily struggle meaning we haven't found any blood or hair samples belonging to a possible assailant. Basically, we've got zilch for physical evidence on this one.

"Now. One of the new developments I've got for you has to do with a potential getaway car. I'm not sure how much stock I put into this but you never know which little nugget might make the case. A guy from Hazel Dell called me up yesterday and told me he'd read about the shooting in the paper and realized that he'd driven right past the residence that evening. When I asked him about the time it turned out it was probably just a few minutes after the shooting. That alone means nothing, but when I questioned him further he said he remembered passing a real shabby looking Nova Hatchback not far from the residence. He said the reason he was able to recall the vehicle so well was because it was tearing down the road, going way over the speed limit and heading west. He said he had no way of knowing if the vehicle may have been coming from the Jenkins' residence or not, but I think it's something to keep an eye on. According to our guy the Hatchback was painted a bright lime green so it shouldn't be too hard to spot out there when you're making your rounds. I've been checking for reports of any stolen vehicles matching that description, but so far nothing's turned up."

The detective flipped his notepad to the next page and said, "What I'm most interested in discussing with you, Tom, is our main suspect. We've got one very strong lead, I think. I don't know about you, but I'm a gambling man, and I'd lay a sizeable wager on Elmer Bugg. I know you know him well and that's why I'm after your opinion on this."

Wilson was shaking his head. "It's not Elmer. I'm not a gambler, but I would bet on that."

Surprise shaped the detective's face.

"I understand why you're suspicious of him," Wilson continued, "but I've known Elmer now for a few years and I can tell you it's not him."

"Really? Because there's an awful lot of red flags attached to this guy. Did you know he'd been torturing animals in his trailer?"

"He wasn't torturing them. He was eating them."

"He was eating rodents?"

"I think that's all that was getting him by."

"Okay . . . Then I imagine you're also aware that Elmer had a history of intruding on the Jenkins' property. Stealing from them."

"He'd nabbed vegetables a few times for sustenance."

"And that he has a long history of mental illness, including bouts of schizophrenia."

"Yeah, I've carried his meds for him."

"And then there's the gun. We got our ballistics report back and the analysis confirmed my hunch. The bullets used to murder Lesley are the same type of rounds typically used in the gun that was stolen on Christmas Day, and which we have every reason to believe was taken by Elmer."

"But we never found that gun. And you know how people are. They tell you all sorts of precious things have been stolen to beef up their insurance claim. I'm sorry, but I believe Elmer. I don't think he took it. I don't even think he'd know what to do with it."

The detective raised his eyebrows and gave the sergeant a look. "Listen, Tom. I don't mean any offense when I say this, but I think maybe you've allowed yourself to get too close to Elmer if you're able to sympathize with him like this. I think if you were looking at this as objectively as I am you'd be coming to the same conclusion as me."

"I'm not saying you shouldn't be doing your due diligence, but I discussed Elmer with Les himself and even he hadn't been worried about him. Elmer's not an aggressive type of person. Yeah, he's got some psychiatric problems. But he's not a murderer."

The sergeant cleared his throat. "Tom, you've been out of the loop on this for a few days and I think you're missing a key element regarding Elmer. He's been missing since the night of the shooting."

"He didn't know that?" the detective said.

"No, I didn't," Wilson said as he took a few moments to digest the information. "I still don't think it's him."

The detective rolled his eyes. "Then maybe you can furnish us with your own expert hypothesis."

"Take it easy, Raymond," the sergeant said.

"Well, what the fuck."

"If it were me I'd be searching for Griswold Frye," Wilson said.

"Griz," said the detective. "And you don't think I already took a hard look at him?"

"I'm not saying you didn't. But if you're looking for someone capable of this level of violence then I think he's your man. He's been prone to assault. And he had a profound grudge against Les. One night he even . . ." Wilson bit off the end of the sentence, knowing it would only sound like speculation and maybe worse. "Griswold was a real threat to Les and Louanne. That's who I'd be looking at."

"And I did," the detective spat. "But you know what? He skipped town a week before the shooting."

"According to who?"

"According to everybody we asked about him. Every one of his family members and all the buddies he'd been running around with said the same thing unequivocally. That he'd gone down to northern California a week before the shooting to visit an old girlfriend of his. Of course, that means he broke his parole and we'll pop him for that, but we got the same story from everyone. Griz was gone. Soon as we can determine exactly where he's been we'll look into verifying whether or not he can prove that he's got a solid alibi. But what we've got on Elmer right now is a hell of a lot more damning and that's where we think we ought to be focusing our efforts and resources."

The sergeant had been brushing some lint off his sleeve and he asked the detective, "Maybe you can answer a question for me, Raymond. If we're all so worried about Elmer now, then why did he get released so soon after this incident on Christmas Day?"

"That's a good question, isn't it. The answer I got was that the public defender worked out a deal for Elmer that if he agreed to move into a sort of halfway house for men struggling with mental issues then he'd get a dramatically reduced sentence. Elmer took the deal but there was a snafu with the house. Something to do with asbestos so the county allowed him to stay at home until they got the place cleaned up. Talk to the sheriff about it if you're curious enough. All these deals are about keeping the jail budget down."

The sergeant shook his head.

"This is the system we have to work with," lamented the detective. "And some good people got shot because of its shortcomings."

"And what about Louanne?" asked the sergeant. "Is there any hope she'll wake up and tell us what all happened?"

"That's a possibility," answered the detective. "But even if she does wake up, and even if her mental faculties are still in order, she'll be considered a highly unreliable witness on account of the Alzheimer's she was beginning to suffer from. It may be a longshot, but we are hopeful we'll get a testimony from her eventually."

"Is there anything else that Tom and I should be aware of?"

"Well, like I said, at the moment we're putting the majority of our resources into locating Elmer and for now that includes extra surveillance of his property by a few deputies we're pulling from west precinct. If I think of anything else I'll give you both a call. Let's all just make sure to keep the communication open between us."

With that the three of them stood.

The detective reached out and took Wilson's hand and he didn't let it go. "You've been through hell," he said. "I can see that clear as day. So you just focus on Mount St. Helens and know that I'm going to put the hurt on this fucker for you."

Wilson nodded and looked away.

"Sergeant Davies. We'll be in touch."

The detective shut the door behind him and the sergeant motioned for Wilson to return to his seat.

"Well," said the sergeant.

"It's not Elmer."

"Perhaps. Tell me why you interrupted yourself earlier?"

"Because I didn't want Raymond to think I was flinging around wild theories."

"Then tell me instead."

"I was at their house one night a few weeks back. Les was away. Louanne was in the bathroom so I answered the phone for her. Somebody called to threaten Les. The voice was distorted, but I'm sure it was Griz."

"And what did Les say when you told him about it?"

Wilson stared blankly.

"I see. So you didn't tell Les, nor did you report a threat against our former sheriff. And considering that, you still expect me to just trust your hunches."

"I don't understand how Raymond can be discounting Griz so easily. Maybe he did skip town a week before the shooting. So what? He could have snuck back without telling anybody. You said it yourself. He's slippery."

"It doesn't compute for me. Yes, Griz had some kind of grudge against Les. Yes, I think he's capable of murder. And I'll even grant you that it was probably him or one of his buddies threatening Les on the phone. But all that being said, I don't see Griz squeezing the trigger on this one. The carelessness of it. The absence of any theft. It doesn't add up for me. I'm inclined to agree with Raymond. I'd also put my money on Elmer."

"Well, will you at least support me if I go hunting after Griz?"

"That I will do. Whether or not he murdered Les, he needs to go away. Besides that, it'll keep you out of Raymond's hair. And it is his show to run. You forget that at your own peril."

Wilson stood.

"Tom?"

"Yeah?"

"You know you can talk to me about anything that's troubling you, right?"

"Sure, Sarge."

"Because I want you to be careful."

"I will."

"I mean, take care of your own head."

Wilson paced along the property line on a dirt trail designed for motorcycles and ATVs. Ahead of him was the owner of this large wooded tract, a bald plumber leading the way atop a mud-splattered quad. The plumber veered around a patch of blackberries and then coasted down a decline as Wilson followed him at a trot to the rear of the property. They stopped at a flimsy wire fence and the plumber killed the engine and lifted himself slowly and sorely from the quad.

"Is this really what she's upset about?" the plumber moaned.

A pile of brush lay gathered into a natural bowl of earth and Wilson walked around inspecting it with mild duty-bound interest.

"What was it she said exactly?" asked the plumber.

"She said that you've been throwing stuff up against her fence."

The plumber gestured to the pile. "Does it look like I've been throwing anything at her property?"

One rogue stick about the size of a walking pole leaned against the fence and poked through six inches to the other side.

"I don't know," Wilson said. "Maybe she means that stick right there."

"Oh my God. Are you serious?"

"That'd be my guess. That's all I'm seeing."

The plumber threw his hands up in the air like he had something imaginary to juggle and said, "That one stinking stick? That's it? It wasn't like I was trying to piss her off. I was just piling up some brush after the storm and it landed like that. I didn't even notice it until now. Why won't she just talk to *me* about this stuff if it bothers her? Why does she gotta go call the police about one stinking stick?"

"It takes all kinds," Wilson said.

"Well, it sure must cause that woman is crazier than a rabid coon. I've lived here for forty years and I never had any problems like this until she moved in. You know she was out here one day taking pictures of me? Yeah. Like she was some private investigator. Back over there hiding in the bushes and spying on me. Can you believe that? I just waved at her."

"Well, let's just get that stick out of her fence."

"Alright. I got it. Didn't even know it was there."

"And while you're at it, pull back that whole pile a few inches. That way she won't have any more cause for complaining."

Afterwards, Wilson followed the plumber back up to his house which sat atop a knoll overlooking the distant timberlands. The plumber slumped into a lawn chair and offered a seat to Wilson who declined. A teenage girl came out to meet them with a cat cradled in her arms and the plumber sent her back inside to fetch them some water.

"Did you feel that earthquake this morning?" the man asked.

"No. I live out in Longview."

"Boy, it really rocked us. I actually thought the mountain had blown at first. The dogs were all barking and the picture frames were rattling against the wall. I was about ready to hit the deck. That earthquake was really something, wasn't it, Daisy?" he asked his daughter as she returned with two glasses of ice water.

"It was kind of exciting," the girl said as she handed off the drinks. "But it was kind of scary too."

"What are we gonna do if the mountain blows?" he asked her.

"Get down into the bomb shelter."

"That's right. Don't worry about none of your stuff. That's just stuff. You run down into that shelter as quick as you can. Maybe grab the cat if you see him but don't risk yourself doing it. That cat's older than he has any right to be." The man took a long thirsty drink and then set his glass aside. "What do you think, Deputy Wilson? You think we ought to be nervous about living right here?"

The girl was eyeing Wilson like his badge made him an expert on such matters and he gave her a comforting smile. "If you've got a bomb shelter then you've got nothing to worry about. The only thing I'd be concerned with is an ash fallout, but that's something you can hunker down and ride out. You guys will be just fine."

The girl was nodding like that was the right answer as Wilson's radio crackled for a response. He took a few steps out of earshot and told the dispatcher to go ahead.

An attempted burglary has been reported at 46 Blackmore Avenue, Yacolt. The suspects were apprehended and are currently being detained by the homeowner. Immediate assistance has been requested.

Wilson passed his water back to the girl and was already backpedaling for his cruiser.

"Godspeed," called the man with a wave.

The address Wilson had been given belonged to a modest tan rambler near the edge of town. Along the front of the house a throng of well-tended rhododendrons bloomed in reds and yellows while up above the mailbox a Confederate flag fluttered with a scant breeze. As Wilson walked up to the stoop a housewife with a mouthful of braces pushed open the screen door and beckoned him inward.

"Thank you for coming, officer. We've been detaining 'em for you."

"They're still inside the house here?"

"Yessir. Come on in and take a look at these hooligans for yourself."

Wilson stepped inside a tidy, lemon-smelling living room that bore the unmistakable motif of white supremacy, one entire wall given to a swastika-emblazoned poster for the National Socialist White People's

Party. In the center of the room was a colorful hand-woven rug and atop this stood a short bony man with a shotgun trained upon two youths sitting dejectedly on the family's couch. One of the boys Wilson didn't recognize. The other was Rodney Vertner.

The man of the house had his back to Wilson but he quartered just enough to throw a few words over his shoulder while keeping the boys in his sights. "Appreciate you getting here so quick. I caught these two scoundrels squirreling around in my shed after I got home from work. They was after my chainsaw and power tools. Thought they could make off with them in broad daylight. How's that for dimwits?"

Wilson gave Rodney a long, hard lookover, but the boy had found a spot on the floor to scowl at and he didn't seem inclined to give it up. His accomplice was a freckled ginger of perhaps fifteen years and he sat in a clump of baggy hand-me-down rags and was returning the glare of the shotgun barrels with a look of continuous terror. Both of the boys appeared twitchy and high.

"I commend you for being so proactive," Wilson said. "But now that I'm here would you mind putting that shotgun away for me."

The man looked like he'd just been asked a great favor and it was with reluctance that he broke the shotgun open, dropped the shells into his coat pocket, and finally hung the weapon back over the kitchen doorframe.

When the man returned he aimed a finger at the boys and said, "These two don't know it but they're pretty goll dang lucky. If I'd known them to be Jews, I probably woulda roughed 'em up first before I called you. And I don't even know what I woulda done if they'd been niggers. Probably wouldn't have even called you at all if you catch my drift."

"I see," Wilson said. "Well, you know I don't condone that type of action."

"Oh, I know you have to say that in your position," the man said with a wink. "Just want you to know we've got your back."

Wilson looked at the boys. "And you're positive these two were attempting to steal your belongings?"

"Well, let's see. When I spotted them, they had the equipment in their hands and were about to walk right out of my shed with the stuff. Considering I don't know who they are, I'd say they were trying to rob me. What do you say?"

"I'd say you've got a pretty solid case there."

"Damn right."

"You boys got anything to say for yourself?" Wilson asked them.

Rodney looked up briefly with the coldness of a viper and back at the floor. His partner slowly raised his hand and he held it aloft in silence until Wilson called on him.

"I didn't want to do it," the boy said pathetically. "He made me."

Rodney glared at the boy but said nothing.

His accomplice began to blubber. "I'm really sorry for what I did. I just want to go home now. Please just let me go back home."

The woman stood watching them with her hands on her hips. She shook her head from side to side like an oscillating fan and said, "It just goes to show you what happens when the parents don't raise their kids with the right values. Just goes to show."

Wilson roused the boys up off the couch and handcuffed one to the other and then ushered them into the backseat of his cruiser. The man and his wife had followed them outside and when Wilson started up the engine the woman hollered for him to hold on for a moment and quickly ran into the house. When she returned she went around to the driver's side window and held out for Wilson two applications for the National Socialist Youth Movement, admissible for white, non-Jewish boys ages fourteen to seventeen.

"This might be what they need," the woman said. "It always kept our boys on the right path. A real stand-up organization."

"Uh-huh."

"We ain't saying we hate. We're just tired of getting stabbed in the back by Jews and niggers."

"Alrighty. Well—"

"Just had a real nice meeting over there in Hazel Dell. Lots of good people getting involved. You oughta come out for the next one."

"Well, I've gotta get going now. I'll call you if we have any more questions."

Wilson stepped on the gas and screeched off before the woman could say any more. They rode in silence for the sheriff's office, long evening shadows beginning to creep across the highway. Wilson had driven halfway to the station when he suddenly punched the steering wheel and jerked the car to a swift stop along the side of the road. He turned around in his seat and sought out Rodney's eyes.

"Look at me," he said.

Rodney continued to stare out his window.

"I said, look at me."

The boy's eyes were red and enflamed and angry.

"You're high, aren't you?"

"No."

"What did you take?"

He wouldn't answer.

"What the hell did you take?"

"Just some stuff we got from a guy."

"What kind of stuff?"

"PCP."

"Jesus Christ, Rodney."

"Will you just keep driving."

"You stupid kid. I can't protect you anymore."

"I never asked you for your help."

"No, but you're gonna wish you had it now. With all the crap that you've been pulling lately. They're gonna look at you like you're a potential murder suspect."

With that Rodney finally showed some interest. "A murder suspect?"

"Yes, Rodney. A murder suspect."

"Sir," the redheaded boy said meekly.

"And now you'll have attempted burglary on your record. A drug charge. All this has to be documented. There's nothing I can do about that. And the detective is gonna come and ask you a bunch of questions about where you were the night of the murder."

"Sir," the boy said again.

"I sure hope you have some good answers for him. Jesus Christ. PCP?"

"Mr. Deputy Sir?"

"Yes, I hear you. What do you need?"

"I've got to go to the bathroom. Really bad."

"You'll just have to hold it until we get to the station."

The boy grimaced and draped his free arm across his knees as Wilson continued driving. On the right they passed a lady on a riding lawn mower who held an arm up in a vague salute as she crossed her field, the smell of cut grass wafting richly through the passenger window. Wilson took up the radio mic and reported his status and hung it back in place. He shook his head.

"How did you two even manage to concoct this sort of nonsense in the first place?"

Rodney was through talking so the redhead answered, "Just bored, I guess."

A slow day for law enforcement. Wilson had already made two thorough laps of his district and now he was working on his third. He kept imagining that he would turn down some quiet road and there with luck he would find Griz. Or Elmer perhaps.

The days since the shooting had begun to blend together, and he felt as though the world had already forgotten about Les and Louanne. All anyone wanted to discuss was the volcano, and would it blow. On the radio that morning a local newscaster had reported that Mount St. Helens was beginning to form an ominous bulge on its north face, an indication of great pressure building within. Good, he thought. Let Cowlitz and Skamania counties deal with the fireworks. In Clark there was a murderer to find.

Wilson drove on through boggy terrain where cows stood chewing their cud in six inches of black mire. His passing engine seemed to upset a flock of tiny birds, and a thousand of them rose up in a black cloud that swung around in unison like a school of harried fish. The morning's drizzle had finally petered out and now the sky was the color of eggshells and faintly luminous. He was nearly to Fargher Lake when the sun pierced through and a rainbow began to paint itself against the distant hills.

When Wilson came to the Christmas tree farm he pulled over and shifted his cruiser to park. He took his time stretching the road-fatigue from his joints and then reached behind the seat to paw around for his lunch sack. Finally, he caught hold of it, and he set the sack in his lap and looked to see what there might be left to snack on.

He was just unwrapping a chocolate bar when a Nova Hatchback roared past in a bright green shimmering streak. Thirty miles an hour over the speed limit, he guessed. Immediately he hit his siren and lights and stomped on the gas. His tires kicked up a spray of gravel and found solid traction and the pursuit was on. Wilson had the pedal to the floor and his Plymouth Fury revved through the gears.

"Let's go!" he bellowed at the car. "Giddyup!"

The road was narrow and winding and the Hatchback's driver seemed to know it well. Wilson's speedometer read sixty, seventy, eighty, and still he wasn't closing the gap. Telephone poles and mailboxes whizzed by like things of the past, the countryside beginning to blur like a watercolor painting in live production. Wilson took a hard corner and then another as he missed a Coca Cola truck by a few narrow inches. The road then straightened into a steep and undulating incline and the Hatchback was two long rises ahead. Wilson rocketed upward feeling washed out of everything impure. He welcomed the rush of adrenaline, his heart galloping, his brain honed. He tossed his lunch sack aside and lifted the radio mic.

"This is Deputy Wilson. I'm currently engaged in a high-speed pursuit. Traveling south on a hundred and nineteenth avenue and about to pass the Mountain View Cemetery. The vehicle is a green Nova Hatchback. Possibly connected to the murder of Lesley Jenkins. Officer may need assistance . . ."

Wilson hung up the mic as the Hatchback climbed the hill and continued unabated through the stop sign. When he crested, there was an exhilarating moment of weightlessness as his cruiser flew through the air alongside the old white church and the cemetery. His tires collided again with the pavement and Wilson hurtled downhill with enough velocity that he was finally able to read the license plate to the dispatcher, adding only a bland description of the driver who sat alone in the vehicle.

They went careening through a hard right corner and kept racing west. Wilson drew as near as he could to the Hatchback's bumper and he took up the loudspeaker mic and commanded for the vehicle to pull over. The driver kept looking back into his own rear seat and Wilson issued another order to stop. Ahead on the left was the View Market and the Hatchback suddenly slowed and its turn signal began blinking and they roared into the parking lot.

Wilson skidded his cruiser to a halt and flung the door open. He crouched behind it with his gun drawn and some onlookers dove back into the little convenience store.

"Come out with your hands up," Wilson instructed.

All at once the driver burst out of the Hatchback, shaking and gibbering like an enraptured evangelist.

"Get down on the ground!" Wilson shouted.

He was watching the man's hands very carefully, and his finger rested on the trigger of his gun. The man looked like nothing more than an insurance salesman and he was still babbling when there came a chilling scream from the backseat of the car, anguished and catlike and diminishing to a moan. Some tortured animal it seemed. A woman perhaps.

"Get down on the ground now!" Wilson repeated.

The driver began bending to his knees and pointing toward the backseat of the Hatchback. Wilson was looking back and forth between the two as a curled foot appeared in the rear window.

"Pregnant," the driver finally managed. "She's pregnant."

Wilson came around his door and when the driver was fully prostrate he stood to one side of him and looked inside the Hatchback. A woman was stretched out upon the backseat and facing him with her legs propped against the inside of the door, her face twisted with misery.

"I'm having this baby right now!" she shrieked.

Wilson stepped right over the man and opened the door. The woman's legs hung in the air exactly where they'd been. She wore a dress that was up to her belly button and the seats were wet and greasy. Since she wasn't wearing any panties, he could see exactly how dilated she'd become. Some hairs that were not hers were already extruding, and she was breathing like she was near the end of a marathon.

"You've gotta help me have this baby," she begged. "I'll never make it to the hospital."

"Okay. Stay calm. Do you have towels or anything?"

"There's a couple blankets in the trunk. Oh lord. Oh lord. This is all his fault."

Wilson turned to the husband who was still lying on the pavement with his hands on his head.

"Get on up and grab your blankets out of the trunk. We're gonna deliver this baby right here."

"Yessir. I'm very sorry about this."

"Just get the blankets."

He turned back to the woman, who was having a contraction and sounding like she was desperately trying to cool down a bite of food.

"Stay calm now. Your husband and I are gonna get you through this."

"That son of a bitch!"

The husband approached with the blankets and when Wilson turned for them he saw how wide-eyed and weak-kneed the sight of his wife in labor was making him.

"Sir. I need you to get on my radio and tell dispatch what's happening. Tell them where we are and that we need a paramedic unit here immediately."

"Where's the radio?"

"It's in my cruiser next to the gear shifter."

"Right. Where we are, what's happening . . ." he muttered as he went away.

Wilson laid the first blanket down underneath the woman the best he could and held on to the second for when it came time to receive the baby. The woman's contraction passed and she quieted down some.

"What's your name?" she asked him.

"Deputy Wilson."

"I mean what's your Christian name?"

"Thomas. Tom."

"Tom, I don't know if I can do this without some painkillers. I never imagined it would feel quite like this."

"We'll get your husband to run in the store and buy you some aspirin when he gets back. Now you just take it easy and relax the best you can."

"I knew something like this was going to happen. I never did want to live so far away."

"You've got me here with you. Are we about to say hello to a boy or a girl?"

"He'll be a boy."

When the husband returned Wilson immediately sent him in to buy aspirin and several bottles of water and the man dashed away again. Soon after he was gone the woman's back bowed and she squeezed hold of the leather head rests and began to howl.

"I think this is it. Oh lord. Ohhhhh. I think this is it."

"Push then. Push."

The woman's legs were quivering against the doorframe. Wilson leaned in with the blanket and began to see the shape of the head.

"Get me through this and I'll name him Thomas."

"Breathe now. Just breathe. Breathe. And push."

The husband reappeared with an armload of water bottles and aspirin. His wife was wailing away and Wilson hollering for her to push. The man glanced over Wilson's shoulder just in time to see his son's head slipping through the birth canal.

"Pass me a water," Wilson called.

He turned to grab a bottle, but the man was unconscious and toppling over backward like freshly felled timber. He landed flat on his back and stayed there, the bottles rolling away from him in five different directions.

"Did he just faint?" the woman shouted.

"Looks like he did."

"That chickenshit. Oh boy. Here he comes!"

"I've got him. Now push. Push. Push."

When Wilson returned to the sheriff's office that evening the events of his day had already blossomed into legend. A handful of deputies were waiting for their shift to begin, and as Wilson entered the briefing room they stood one by one and applauded, Shef and Troy and the giant and a few others clapping in reverence like he was some great hero returned. Wilson tried his best, but he couldn't help but smile.

Troy reached out and shook Wilson's hand. "You the man," he rasped.

"Is it true they're going to name the baby after you?" Shef asked.

"That's what the mother told me."

"Amazing. That's a real honor, Tom."

"Yeah, especially cause the baby's a little girl," joked one of the deputies.

"Get the man his reward," another hollered out.

The giant walked up with one arm tucked behind his back, grinning like the devil himself. "Close your eyes."

"What do you got, Charles?"

"Nope. I said close 'em."

Expecting trickery, Wilson reluctantly obeyed.

"Alright, you can open 'em now."

The giant held a fat cigar wrapped up in a baby blue string. Wilson took the gift and looked around at all his ebullient brothers in arms. "Wow. Thanks, guys."

"Sergeant got that for you," the giant said.

"Where's he at? I should thank him."

"He's in his office. I think he's on the phone."

Wilson walked across the briefing room fielding handshakes along the way. He knocked on the sergeant's door. The sergeant had the receiver to his ear and a frown clouding his face. He held up a finger and Wilson took a seat.

"Yep. Yep. Alright. Well, I appreciate the call." The sergeant hung up the phone and took a deep breath.

"What's that about?" Wilson asked.

"Oh. Let's talk about it tomorrow."

"What?"

The sergeant shook his head. "It's gonna ruin your night."

Wilson ran his hand through his hair and signified that he was ready.

"That was the warden at the juvenile detention center. Rodney hung himself this afternoon. He's dead."

Something akin to defeat washed over Wilson.

"I'm sorry, Tom. I know you'd been doing a lot to help the kid."

"Does his dad know yet?"

"I'm not sure."

"I should be the one to tell him."

"No, you get home and get some rest. You've had an enormous day."

"Goddamnit, Rodney," Wilson said softly.

"He was a troubled kid. You did everything you could for him."

"What a terrible way to die. In a facility like that."

"I'm confident he's in a better place now."

Wilson looked up at the ceiling and back to the sergeant. "Did he leave a note?"

"Yeah."

"What did it say?"

"It said, I didn't kill nobody."

"Except himself."

"Yeah."

I t was three hours past dinnertime when Wilson finally returned home, and he came listing through the front door smelling of whiskey and smoke. Ellen had been on the phone in the living room and when she saw him she exhaled with relief and rose laboriously from the loveseat holding onto her humongous belly with one hand.

"Yeah, it's him," she said into the phone. "I don't know. I said, I don't know. I've got to go, Mom. I'll call you tomorrow."

Wilson was putting his things away clumsily in the hall closet and Ellen came around to watch him.

"You're drunk," she said.

He looked at her from under a pair of baggy eyelids and said nothing.

"Can't you at least call me? I've been here imagining all sorts of horrible scenarios. I almost called Sergeant Davies."

He staggered past her toward the kitchen.

"And what is that all over your pants?" she asked.

"I slipped in some mud."

"Good Lord, Thomas. You drove home this way?"

"Let me be."

"That's a fine thing to ask when you're like this. I suppose you're hungry too."

"Yeah."

"Well, you can go on and heat it up for yourself then."

He rummaged through the fridge and removed a glass dish. "Is this it?"

"That's it. That was supposed to be our dinner together."

Wilson put the dish into the microwave and stood there holding the counter and watching the machine hum.

"And I'm especially upset because we were supposed to decide on the color scheme for the baby's new room tonight. Now we're not going to be able to get the paint until Monday."

Wilson was shaking his head.

"What? Why are you shaking your head like that?"

He wheeled around with exasperation and a bit of a slur. "For Christ's sake, Ellen. It doesn't matter what color we paint the baby's room."

"How can you say that? How can you say it doesn't matter?"

"The color of the walls is not going to make one bit of difference to you or me or the baby. It's paint. Just leave it the way it is. Or paint it bright teal. Or chartreuse or flaming pumpkin. Paint it with zebra stripes if you like. It doesn't matter. I don't care."

She looked like she'd been wounded terribly and she said, "I don't like you this way. You're drunk and you're acting mean."

"Mean?" he snorted. "You have no idea what mean is. If decorating the baby's room is your biggest concern right now then you'd better count your lucky stars because you've got it made in the shade."

The microwave dinged and Wilson removed the dish and took it over to the dining table where he commenced to wolf the food down. Ellen stared at him in a miasma of hostile silence.

"What is this about?" she asked.

He glanced up over his bowl and forked another heap of food into his mouth.

"Because I can understand if you're having trouble coping with things. Between the shooting and the mountain, you've been under tremendous strain. I just wish you wouldn't come home and take it out on me. I signed up to be your wife, not your punching bag."

Wilson dropped his fork and pushed his bowl aside. "You know what I did today? You know what I was doing while you were fretting over color schemes and cooking beef stroganoff? I was delivering a baby from the backseat of a car."

"Is that true?"

"Yes. A couple were on their way to the hospital and they weren't going to make it and I helped them deliver their baby."

She took the seat across from him at the table. "That's incredible."

"It was incredible. It was totally incredible. I got to hand this little boy off to his mother and I thought, this is why I'm a cop. This right here.

And then you know what happened? I got back to the office and found out from Sergeant Davies that Rodney Vertner hung himself in his juvie cell."

With that Ellen felt the last of her anger and confusion dissipate. She sighed and said, "That's very sad."

"He was a knucklehead, but he wasn't a bad kid. I thought I was making a difference, but it didn't matter. I failed him."

"Don't say that."

"I've been failing. And when I fail, people die."

Outside on the street a car alarm began whooping and Wilson looked in its direction and kept on gazing through the window.

"You're not being fair to yourself," she said. "And when you're not fair to yourself, you're not fair to me either. It's not right to focus on all the rough parts like you are. You can't scrutinize every little thing you might have said or done differently. You've got to weigh it all together and know that you're doing your best."

He scratched at the mud caked along his pantleg.

"Do you need to talk to somebody?" she asked.

"Who would I talk to?"

"I don't know. There must be somebody. I think you should think about it."

Wilson gave her a few guarded looks and then lifted himself up with what seemed like a huge effort. "I'm too tired for this right now."

Without another word he stumbled off toward the bathroom and Ellen watched him go as a visceral sense of dread began to coil around her heart, some sourceless premonition that more bad tidings were galloping fast for her front door. Sitting there she recalled her mother's warnings about the lot of a lawman's wife, the cautionary tales gone unheeded. In some ways, it was harder than she'd ever supposed. The tragedies of life passed on from one person to the next until they arrived in her home like the most unwelcomed of guests. To feast upon her marriage. And rob her of the peace she so desired.

Sometimes she imagined he worked in the mills, came home bored. Other times she imagined her life if she'd married another one of her classmates. The rich dentist. The gym teacher. There were simpler men to love. And yet, despite the fearful nights and the secondhand horrors, she knew that if her life could be replayed a thousand times she would always choose him. If that was the same thing as destiny, then she guessed she was a believer after all.

When she'd finished her tea, she realized she hadn't heard the shower running and she padded over and pushed open the bathroom door. Wilson lay naked in the bathtub. His eyes were shut and his arms were folded across his chest and he'd just begun to snore. He seemed to be comfortable where he was so she went into their bedroom and returned with a pillow and two quilts. The first quilt she draped over Wilson so that he was covered up to his chin, and the other she swaddled around herself. Then she folded her pillow in half, set it down on the linoleum, and curled up to sleep beside him.

Wilson awoke from a deep voidlike stupor. His mouth was chalk dry and for several strange moments he had no idea where he was. He sat upright in the bathtub and looked down at the quilt, slowly piecing together what must have happened the night before. Duke lay on the floor next to him, and as Wilson worked the kinks from his neck the dog began thumping his tail against the toilet.

"Hey there, pooch," Wilson said.

The dog leapt to his paws and jumped up to hang his two front legs over the edge of the tub. Wilson reached out to scratch him behind his ear and Duke's tongue gave way to gravity, drooping with pleasure.

"Go fetch me some water, will ya."

Duke barked, and barked again. Wilson heard Ellen hollering for the dog from the kitchen and Duke bucked up from the tub and trotted away. Eventually Wilson managed to heave himself to his feet. He pulled on some shorts and lumbered out to the living area.

Ellen and Maggie were already eating, the little girl riding high in her booster seat and nibbling the end off a piece of bacon. Wilson loaded himself a plate and sat and took up a fork. He glanced across at Ellen and their eyes met briefly and then fell apart.

Maggie looked up from her food. "Daddy?"

"Chew your food and swallow first."

She did. "Daddy?"

"Yes, dear."

"Can I sleep with you in the bathtub tonight?"

"No."

"Why not?"

"Because it's only for special occasions."

Ellen started to say something but managed to hold on to it. Wilson began hurrying through his meal.

"Daddy?" she asked again.

"Yes, dear."

"Can I be a policeman when I grow up?"

How innocently she awaited his reply, her eyes like a pair of pure blue gems before they've been cut.

"No," he said.

"Because I'm a girl?"

"No. Because you want to have nice dreams."

"Oh."

When he was finished with breakfast Wilson went and got his jacket and wallet and truck keys. He was heading for the door when Ellen looked up from the dishwasher she'd been loading.

"Are you going somewhere?" she asked.

"There's somebody I need to go see."

"Tom, we need to talk about last night."

"I promise I'll look at the paint samples with you as soon as I get home."

"It's not about that."

"I see. Well, we can talk about it later maybe."

"Thomas . . ."

Wilson shut the door behind him and walked out to his truck. It was a balmy and fragrant spring day and the neighbor kids two doors down were running circles in their yard, giddy and screeching.

He drove along Lake Sacajawea and parked across from St. John's Hospital. With some trepidation he crossed the street and walked into the lobby. Behind the reception desk sat a beautiful cat-eyed woman who looked up from a file and smiled.

"Hi," Wilson said. "Can you tell me which room Louanne Jenkins is in?"

As he waited for her to locate the information Wilson turned and nodded at a young man in a soiled baseball uniform who held what appeared to be a dislocated shoulder. The young man grimaced back.

"Okay. Here we are," the woman said. "Are you a member of the family, sir?"

"Not exactly."

"Well, I'm very sorry, but it says that she's in a restricted room. Only her immediate family is being allowed visitation right now."

Wilson showed her his badge and explained his connection to the shooting. "It's very important for me to see her. Is there anyone else I can speak with about being allowed into her room?"

The woman took Wilson's badge and driver's license and looked them over carefully. Then she passed them back and said, "She's in room 332. There's a guard posted outside the door. You'll have to talk to him and see what he says."

Wilson took the stairs to a bright fluorescent hallway. Ahead of him an orderly was wheeling a squabbling gurney along and Wilson followed a few paces behind reading the numbers on the doors. He turned a sharp corner and very nearly collided into Doug who shuddered with surprise.

"Jesus. Tom. Hey. What's going on?"

"Hey, Doug. Just came by to see how your grandma was doing."

Doug looked like he'd been sleeping poorly and drinking a great deal. He was putting on weight and his hair was growing out unattended. "Yeah, I just got done visiting her. She's still sleeping. Same thing every day. I keep coming in and hoping she'll maybe recognize my voice or something but . . . Who knows? None of the doctors can say what'll happen."

Wilson pointed down the hall at a burly old man seated in a plastic chair. "Is that the guard right there?"

"Hank? Yeah, that's him. I'm not sure if he'll let you in though."

"Well. I'll see what he says. Good to see you, Doug." Wilson started to move down the hall.

"Hey, Tom."

He turned.

"I sold the tavern."

"Yeah, I heard that."

"And I decided to move back to California. Thought maybe you didn't know that part. I'm through with Washington. I don't care if I ever see this state again. Nothing but a nightmare for me here."

"Can't say I blame you. I hope you have better luck down there."

"Me too."

"See you around, Doug."

Wilson went down the hall, approaching the guard as he was struggling mightily to get the proper crease into his newspaper.

"Are you Hank?" Wilson asked.

The guard lowered his paper and looked Wilson up and down. "Maybe. Who are you?"

"I'm Tom Wilson. Clark County Deputy Sheriff." He showed the guard his badge. "I was close friends with Louanne. I mean, I still am. The lady at the reception desk said I should talk to you about getting in the room to see her."

"Are you involved with the investigation?"

"I am."

The guard dropped his paper to the floor and stood. "Well. I don't know what good it'll do ya, but I suppose I can let you in for a short visit."

"I really appreciate that."

"But only if you promise not to touch anything. Including her."

"Sure thing."

"I mean it. Don't touch a thing. That guy that just left bumped into something one day and the doctor was pissed as hell. Chewed me out like it was my fault somehow."

"What did he bump into?"

"I don't know. Just some fancy whatchamacallit."

"I won't touch a thing."

"That's right."

The guard unlocked the deadbolt and the door and pushed it open. Wilson peered inside the small dark room. Louanne lay in the bed half enshadowed and hooked up to several machines.

"Go on," the guard said. "I'll give you ten minutes or so."

Wilson stepped inside and the door clanged shut and locked behind him. For a long while he could do nothing but stand there like a sentinel among the smell of antiseptic and the incessant purring of the machines. Louanne's head was wrapped in gauze and bandages but otherwise she looked as though she were merely taking a nap.

He had not anticipated how much the sight of her could disturb him. A sickening swell of emotion churned his innards and he felt his stomach curdle. Frantically he lurched into the bathroom, gripping the sides of the toilet and retching until he had nothing left. After it was over he groaned and rose and washed his mouth out in the sink. Then he looked at himself in the mirror, and it was a bedraggled version reflected back, but it was still him.

When he was ready he pulled up a chair and sat down next to Louanne's bed. How strange, he thought, that she didn't even know she was a widow. Her dreams must be filled with images of a dead man. And then he was crying. Convulsing. Muffling himself with his arm. And she could not console him.

"I'm so sorry," he choked. "It was my fault. I didn't warn Les. I thought I was saving him from worry but he needed to know so he could protect you. I was so careless. So stupid."

Wilson stood and leaned over the bed, dripping hot tears onto her blanket.

"Please wake up, Louanne. Please wake up and forgive me."

There came a knock on the door and Wilson was wiping his face as the guard unlocked the bolt and stepped inside.

He looked curiously at Wilson. "Everything alright in here? You need a few more minutes?"

"No, I've gotta leave."

Wilson took one final look at Louanne and then strode past the guard without another word. The guard followed him out the door and watched him languish down the hall until Wilson was around the corner and out of sight. Then the guard shrugged, locked the door, and sat down again with his newspaper.

Wilson swung some slick branches aside and began taking the footpath down to the river. He still had some time left of his lunch break and he wanted to see how the fish were running. The afternoon was dark and forlorn and the cover of the forest made it more so, the wooded quietude only interrupted by cars passing periodically on the road above. Wilson walked briskly down the damp pungent trail, hopping over roots and rivulets and the trash discarded by anglers and skinny dippers and the occasional truant. He made a final leap from the eroded bankside and landed with a crunch upon the gravelly shore.

There was no one fishing that portion of river. Or if there had been they'd given up already. The faintest of all mist was falling and Wilson could just feel it on his neck and on the back of his hands, yet he could not spot even a dimple in the river where it must be landing. He stepped out toward the gurgling water until his boot toes were wet and then filled himself with the sylvan serenity. The ceaseless transit of that tributary like a mantra in motion.

It wasn't long before he spotted a fair-sized Chinook salmon gliding upstream in a shallow side channel. The fish seemed to be in no great hurry. It only flapped its caudal fin here and there, and it swam in such low water that Wilson could see its speckles and its ugly hooked snout as it passed along to spawn and die. He watched two other salmon more urgent about their travels and then he picked up a handful of rocks and tossed them plunking into some riffles as he walked along the river's edge.

Around the second bend he came upon a fisherman. An old Indian he'd seen passing through town a few times. The Indian had his back and long gray ponytail turned and he was just throwing a cast upstream. There was a splash some thirty yards distant and Wilson watched him work the line to keep it taut and to give the bait action as it drifted back toward him and then on down the river while he played the spool. Once he'd reeled in his line he rotated and planted his feet and cast once more. Wilson watched him cast four times and then hollered howdy.

The Indian reeled in and faced him with a wary look, a deep fissured scar running from his ear to the corner of his mouth. "Which regulation am I breaking this time?"

"Oh, I'm not here about that."

"Warden didn't send you after me?"

"No."

"Then what other kind of bad news you got for me?"

Wilson put his hands up. "Relax. Nothing's the matter. I'm just here to see if the fish are biting."

The Indian studied Wilson for another moment and then finally relaxed. He set his rod down on the rocks and walked over and opened a wicker creel and tilted it in Wilson's direction. Inside was a salmon big enough that it needed bending to fit.

Wilson whistled. "You got some good eating to look forward to."

"Yeah. Only wish I could find another just like him."

"What sort of bait you using?"

The Indian closed the basket and looked at him out of the corner of his eye. "You sure you're not trying to get me for something?"

"I promise I'm just an ignorant fisherman."

The Indian nearly smiled. "Best thing to use is their own eggs. Wrap 'em up in a little bundle and fasten it to the hook. The rottener the eggs the better."

Wilson thanked him and they both looked out toward the river. On the opposite bank a heron was wading in the mud and it took a long slow step and bent its beak to the water and waited.

"Well," said Wilson. "Is this mountain going to blow up on us or not?"

"I'm sure of it."

"How's that?"

The Indian didn't seem to hear the question. He'd been studying the clouds to the north and he said, "Do you know what some of my people are saying about it?"

"No."

"They're saying that the mountain is angry. Lawelatla, my people call it. They say that the mountain is acting for our people and that the eruption will be divine retribution for what the white man has done to our spirits. For desecrating our ancestors' graves. For building dams over our sacred places. For stealing the bones of our grandmothers and carting them off to museums."

"I guess if I were in their shoes I might feel the same way."

The Indian shook his head. "To me such talk is only superstition. Many of their beliefs I don't share anymore and so we get into fights. They tell me I've forsaken my heritage. But some of them refuse to learn the science, refuse to change. I tell them, why should white people take us seriously when we hang on to such myths?"

Wilson wondered if he was being trapped. "I don't know. They could be right."

"I don't think so. That mountain is not interested in getting revenge for my people. That mountain is only a volcano. And volcanoes erupt. My grandfather told of seeing the last eruption with his own eyes. And there were many more eruptions before that. Where were the white men then? Why should they get to take credit for everything?"

Wilson chuckled.

"That doesn't make what the white man did to us right. But who can say what we would have done to your folks if things had been the other way around. We weren't savages. But we weren't angels neither. My grandfather told me many stories that confirmed that."

"I can see why you get into a lot of arguments."

"Yeah. But I'm tired of fighting all the time. I'm an old man and I want to be happy. For me that mostly means fishing."

"Well, I hope you get another big one. I'd better get running along."

The Indian waved and Wilson headed back down the river. He was halfway around the first bend when he lurched at the sound of an enormous blast, a deep raucous percussion as loud as a truckload of dynamite detonated from just across the creek. Then the ground began shuddering beneath his very boots and a panicky terror swept through him as another even louder blast seemed to rip the sky at its seams. He knew it could only be the mountain and when he looked back for the Indian he saw that the old fisherman was already gone. Wilson took off sprinting for his car.

D eputies were in short supply and Wilson had agreed to work late, his mind so restless he'd in fact welcomed the extra hours on the road. Deep into the night he ruminated on the mountain and the murderer. One still clearing its throat, the other in hiding.

The lightning storm proved a good distraction. Every now and again the tops of the trees would show their outline against a purple flash of sky and he would count out until he heard thunder, the roar of the heavens growing loud and louder. When he rolled back into Yacolt he parked his car downtown and stepped out into the road. There was no traffic, no one about. Only a mangy housecat was active and Wilson watched it stalk down the sidewalk and disappear under a hedge. Above the gas station the crescent moon was rising like some ivory horn, and a glitter of drizzle tumbled to the pavement in a wash of lamplight. Wilson stood in marvel of the streets. This midnight melancholy of sleeping citizens. All his to secure.

He had just lit up a cigarette when an indigo zag fractured the sky overhead. The thunder rolled in quickly, sounding like desperate cannonfire from some bloody field of revolution. More lightning soon showed there and there and he flinched and ducked for all the good it would do him. The thunder seemed to crash upon his very car and a cacophony of neighborhood dogs began to howl out their disdain. Wilson puffed on his cigarette, and as he watched for more in the expectant silence he felt like a young boy razzed into false bravado.

"Come on and get me," he told the lightning.

The storm did pass and eventually Wilson received a call. A woman had reported seeing strange shadows moving outside her window and was asking for someone to check for burglars. Wilson drove on toward the residence expecting to find nothing but paranoia.

The home was but a plain, double-wide trailer near Chelatchie and it sat away from the road on a large secluded property with a sign on the gate that read *TRESPASSERS WILL BE VIOLATED!* Wilson walked up to a porch littered with cigarette butts and knocked twice. A moment later the door opened to show a dough-faced blonde wearing a loose white night dress that ran out of fabric just below her crotch.

"Oh," she said. "You're not Henry."

"No, I'm not."

She was looking him over with bold curiosity as Wilson leaned back and peered upon the yard. "You said you saw some shadows out here that were worrying you?"

"That's right."

"And did you hear any voices or strange noises to go along with them?"

"No. Just the shadows."

"Whereabouts did you see them?"

"Well, I saw them from my bedroom. Let me show you."

She turned and sashayed into the rear of the home, her abundant posterior rippling against the scanty fabric. Wilson paused and then followed her inside.

"Mama," a young voice called from within a bedroom.

"Go back to sleep," the woman said.

Her bedroom was sloppy with discarded clothes and smelled of stale smoke and cloying incense. An orange shag carpet furred the floor and a lava lamp slowly oozed atop the dresser. She went around behind her bed and pulled the blinds.

"I was seeing them right out there by the wading pool."

Wilson looked. "I'm not seeing anything unusual."

"You can't see them from over there. You'll have to come around."

He hesitated.

"Come on around. I see one now."

Wilson stepped over a pair of panties and stood alongside her.

"There's one," she said. "You see it?"

"That's your lawn gnome."

"Not that. The one that's moving."

"That's just a tree. The wind's playing with it."

"But there were others before. Spooky ones."

"I don't know what to tell you, ma'am. Is it just you and your child living here?"

"My husband's away for the week," she said in a contrived starlet's voice. "And I get so scared and lonesome when I'm here all by myself."

"Well . . ."

"Since you're here could you please help me with something else?"

"I do have other calls I need to get to."

"Henry was always *very* good about helping me when my husband was away."

"What do you need?"

"I'm just trying to move my bed."

"Right now?"

"Only a foot or two. So that the light doesn't shine on it so early in the morning."

"Okay. But then I've really got to get going."

He went around to the other side of the bed and took hold. When he looked up he saw that she'd leaned over and was gazing at him with what she thought was a slatternly advantage, her enormous naked breasts hanging almost entirely out of the gaping neck of her night dress.

Wilson looked down at the bed. "Let's get it moved."

He lifted and the woman pushed and they got the bed to where she wanted it. Wilson straightened up and watched as the woman then tumbled onto the mattress, her dress up around her belly button.

"You see something you like," she said while playing her legs like a cello.

"Ma'am. This is unseemly."

"Don't be afraid. I can be very discreet."

"I'm not afraid. I'm married."

"So was Henry and it never bothered him too much."

"Well, I'm not Henry."

She winked at him. "No. You're not."

"Don't ever call dispatch again unless you have a real problem," he said as he turned for the door.

She sat up, stunned and furious. "What are you? A fucking queer?"

Wilson was going through the home when he noticed a young sleepy-eyed girl of about seven half-hiding behind her bedroom door.

"What's going on?" she asked.

"Everything's okay. Try to go back to sleep."

"Fuck you. Don't talk to my kid," the woman shouted.

It was tempting to tell the woman exactly what he thought of her, but he looked again at the child and then simply closed the door behind him. An emergent rain had begun falling and Wilson hurried behind the wheel of his cruiser. As he was backing out of the driveway the woman's face appeared in one of the trailer's living room windows. She scowled and threw the curtains shut and the light was extinguished.

Wilson turned back toward town as his windshield wipers thumped and wicked the falling water aside. He passed a few large pastures all blanketed in fog and soon came alongside the abandoned plywood mill. In the dark and the rain, it looked like some warehouse of broken promise, and as there was nothing pressing to attend to he made the corner and pulled up to the mill entrance.

Management had given him a key and he stepped out and unlocked the gate. Then he continued inside with his lights off and his windows rolled down. He could hear frogs croaking out by the mill pond and the surroundings smelled of mud and greasy machinery. At a crawl he proceeded past an assortment of gray buildings and conveyer belts and heavy equipment that had yet to be liquidated. It was hard to envision now, but hundreds of locals had been employed here just last spring. Wilson reflected on all the laid-off workers he knew who were still looking for jobs, their families still struggling. As soon as the trees had run out, the management folded up and vanished like some traveling circus. It was an old trick, and it had happened here before.

He drove on toward the center of the complex. Here and there he spotted graffiti on the outbuilding walls, some of it freshly tagged, some of it beyond derogatory. He checked his rearview mirror, and his eyes were just leaving it when he caught sight of a dark hunched figure loping across the road. Human or animal, he could not tell.

Wilson slammed on the brakes and shifted to reverse, his cruiser whining as it undid its progress. He flicked on his spotlight and its powerful moonbeam carved a shifting tunnel as he worked it back and forth across a decrepit forklift and a heap of scrap metal. He was radioing dispatch his situation when the figure stood up from behind an oil drum and took off sprinting deeper into the mill grounds. Wilson quickly called for backup and then flung himself from the car to give chase.

"Police!" he shouted. "Stop right there!"

Wilson was about a hundred yards behind and he was splashing up mud puddles with every third or fourth step. As he ran, his flashlight was skipping around and losing, alighting, losing this mysterious absconder. Wilson followed as the man hurdled a stack of steel bars, ran straight through the boiler house, and went on around the corner of the crane shed. When Wilson spotted him next, the man had clambered up a makeshift ladder and was halfway through a second-story window of the plywood factory.

For a moment Wilson hesitated to follow. But as there were so many potential exits, he reluctantly climbed up the buckling ladder. When he reached the top, he clicked on his flashlight and shone it inside the window. He just caught a glimpse of the man's heels as he ducked around a far wall, and then he could hear the man's footsteps go rapping off into some shadowy corner. Wilson squeezed through the window and dropped onto an elaborate metal catwalk that overlooked the factory floor.

He drew his gun, cocked the hammer, and listened. The rain was making a ruckus on the roof above, but as far as he could tell the footsteps had quit.

"I don't know who you are, and I don't know why you're running," Wilson hollered, his voice echoing from wall to wall. "But there's a murderer on the loose in this area. So I'm not gonna be thinking twice before I shoot. Come on out now. Nice and easy."

Wilson waited. There came no reply. In the best of circumstances, his backup was probably still ten or fifteen minutes away. He couldn't afford to make any mistakes.

Onward he crept along the catwalk, his flashlight and gun each swaying slightly from side to side. Rain was leaking from a few small holes in the roof and landing with loud plops at his feet. Finally, he reached a sharp blind corner, the last spot where he'd heard the man's footsteps. He took a deep breath. And another in preparation. Then he turned and aimed both his gun and flashlight. There was nothing but a dark stairway leading to the main floor.

He considered everything for a few moments and began to take the stairs. Each step afforded him new angles of the pallets and machinery and he took his time the whole way. When he finally reached the bottom, Wilson paused and shined the flashlight back and forth across the factory floor. There was absolutely no sign of the man, and he was dispirited to notice two open doors leading back outside. The man had surely fled. Only an imbecile would still be hiding somewhere inside.

Wilson began heading back toward his car. Just before the door he stopped and fought with the air and cursed. When that was done, he breathed out his disappointment and looked up into the rafters.

"Unbelievable," he said.

Twenty feet up on a dusty beam, Elmer clung like some mutant opossum.

"Get down out of there," Wilson said.

"You'll have to come get me."

"Get down out of there now or I'm going to shoot you."

There was a moment of indecision. Wilson aimed his gun square at Elmer's chest and then he said, "Alright."

If he'd always looked horrible before then Elmer looked even horribler now. He was starving and sallow and covered in filth. Wilson led him back to his car in handcuffs like some ghoulish specimen bound for the freak show. At the cruiser Wilson guided him carefully into the backseat and passed him what few things he had to eat.

Elmer devoured the food loudly and grossly. When he was finished, he said, "You've got to let me go."

Wilson had been watching him. "You really must be crazy."

"Yeah, but it's not my fault."

"Did you shoot Les and Louanne?"

"No."

He asked it again more forcefully. "Did you shoot Les and Louanne?"

"No. I've never even touched a gun."

"Then why have you been hiding out all this time?"

"Because I knew everybody would think I'd done it."

"And now they're sure you did it."

"But I didn't. How could I shoot them? Them and you were the only ones that was ever kind to me."

Wilson took some time to ponder that.

"Please let me go," Elmer said pathetically. "I'll catch a bus to another state. I'll go to Idaho. Or Alaska. Nobody'll miss me."

"I can't do it, Elmer."

"Please."

"I can't. They'd fire me or worse if they found out."

Elmer took to whimpering some. "They're gonna hang me. They're gonna frame me and hang me."

"I won't let that happen."

"You ain't a judge."

"No, but—"

"And you ain't a jury. So you can't save me except by letting me go."

"How can I know you didn't shoot them in some schizophrenic delusion and not even know you'd done it? How could I know that I'd be doing the right thing?"

"Because you know me. You know that I'm crazy, but I'm not evil. Just look at me. Do I look like a murderer?"

Wilson shook his head. "That's the wrong question to ask, Elmer. To a lot of people, you do."

"But do *you* think I did it?"

After some reflection Wilson said, "I suppose I don't."

"Then you've got to let me go. Take me to the bus station right now and you'll never hear from me again. Please. Please help me. I'm not a murderer."

Wilson chewed on the inside of his lip, thinking hard about what he could and couldn't live with. Then he started up the car and drove on into the rain.

After two weeks of dormancy, St. Helens was once more shuddering and spewing ash. The earthquakes had been the largest yet, and airplane pilots were warned to avoid a six hundred square mile area on account of the gritty volcanic particles and what they could do to an engine. Once again, the most apprehensive locals were considering extended vacations.

Wilson pulled into the parking lot of Dolores' place and came to a stop alongside another police cruiser. He stepped out and beheld an eerie, gray noon. The mountain was not visible for the clouds, but its sooty emanations were being carried by the wind to slowly drift and dust and ashen the spring day ominous. The citizenry seemed surprisingly unconcerned. Errand-bound pedestrians appeared less worried about the fallout than simply lethargic and longing for the sun. Wilson watched a young boy scoop a handful of ash from the hood of a broken-down car and then he ambled toward the restaurant.

Inside the diner, he was pleased to find Shef seated at the corner table, with his back to the wall and facing the entrance just as Wilson had tutored. Shef nodded and Wilson pulled out a chair next to him.

"How you enjoying our weather?" Wilson asked.

"I wish the sucker would just go on and blow its wad already. I'm sick of this gloom."

"I thought you grew up on this side of the state? Should be pretty used to it by now."

"Rain's one thing. This is like Armageddon."

"Armageddon? We haven't even gotten started on that yet. Hey, did you order me a burger already?"

"Dolores oughta be cooking it now."

"You tell her to hold the pickles?"

"Shoot. My bad."

Over his shoulder, Wilson hollered for the kitchen. "Say, Dolores. You mind holding those pickles for me?"

A huge pink head in a hairnet poked through the kitchen window. "I gotcha, honey. When someone says it's for Deputy Wilson they don't need to say nothing about holding the pickles. I know you'd just throw 'em back at me."

"Thanks, Dolores."

"You boys sit tight. Food'll be right up."

Wilson thrummed his fingers on the table.

"You look better than the last few times I saw you," Shef said.

"That isn't saying very much."

"How you holding up?"

Wilson shrugged. "I'm still not sleeping more than a few winks a night. I'm not getting along with my wife. And I think I might have helped send an innocent man away to prison for the rest of his life so I . . ."

Their food was on its way and they sat back as the waitress slid their plates in front of them. Wilson leaned forward and lifted the bun from his burger.

"What's the deal? Dolores just said she was holding the pickles."

He turned toward the kitchen and Dolores cackled tremendously and ducked back out of sight.

The waitress grinned and switched their plates. To Wilson she said, "That woman loves you."

Wilson splattered ketchup over his fries and they began eating.

"So hold on," Shef said. "You're saying you still don't think it was Elmer who did it?"

"Maybe I'm the one that's crazy. No. I don't think he did it."

"But they must have a pretty strong case against him. The prosecutor already pressed charges. He'll be arraigned next week."

"That's what I hear. They can't get a confession out of him though, can they?"

"Come on, Tom. I was there with you on Christmas Day when he broke into that family's home and stole their gun. The guy's a total wack job. You never know what a guy like that might do. For Christ's sake, he was filleting rodents. You carried his psycho drugs for him."

"But they still can't find that gun."

"So what? He could have dumped it anywhere."

Wilson set his burger down and swallowed. "Don't you ever have gut instincts about things?"

"Yeah. And they're usually wrong."

"I thought you just started four months ago? You already sound like the lieutenant."

Shef wiped his mouth with his napkin and sat back in his chair. "So what are you saying? You still think it's this Griz guy?"

"Let's just say I'd sleep a lot easier if they found him before they pin all this on Elmer. Seems odd that he still hasn't shown up yet."

"Hell, I'd be hiding out too if I was in his shoes. Even if I was innocent."

"Yeah, well. Maybe I'm wrong. But I can't get that phone call out of my head. And everything Lesley told me about Griz. It eats at me."

"I hear you, man. You and Lesley were good friends. You want to see him avenged. And I'm sure it must be hard to believe that the person that killed him might be someone you actually like instead of a real shitbag like Griz. But you've got to try and put your faith in the system. Detective

Depp and the prosecutor and everybody else want justice just as badly as you do."

Wilson looked up and shook his head. "No, they don't. Not even close."

The restaurant was beginning to fill up with the typical lunchtime crowd and Wilson watched the loggers and ranchers and retirees slap each other's backs and joke their jovial howdys.

Ferlin Blackstone soon appeared at the entrance and he seemed to be searching for someone. When his eyes alit on the deputies, Wilson realized he'd been looking for them. Ferlin bumped through a chittering gaggle of grandmothers and hurried over to their table.

"How you doing, Ferlin?" Wilson asked. "Spot any Sasquatches lately?"

"It's been a little slow. Won't lie about that. Say, how'd you like my book?" he asked Shef.

"Great. Great. Some real good info there."

"What were your favorite parts?"

"Oh. Well. Just the whole thing. I mean—"

"You look like you've got something for us," Wilson intervened. "What's on your mind?"

Ferlin leaned in conspiratorially. "I found another squatter. Out on DNR land. This one seems quite promising to say the least."

Wilson felt his blood quicken. "Did you get a look at the guy?"

"No. But he's spooked about something. I know that much. Here's what happened. I was out . . ."

He silenced himself as the waitress came and dropped the check. She looked around at the three of them hunkered into their intrigue and abruptly turned. Ferlin glanced here and there and then lowered to tell the story.

"I was out on one of my usual forays yesterday evening. You know, scouting around for those hairy devils like I do. I'd driven in there pretty far and then I got out to hunt by foot. Down in the back of this unit there's an old CCC cabin that I'd discovered way back when. A real shithole. Half rotten and full of mouse turds. I've hiked through there a few times since then and the cabin's always been empty. Once it looked like a hunter had maybe stayed for a few nights, but nothing too permanent. I mean, we're talking about some pretty creepy territory out there. I wouldn't even go near it alone unless I was packing some formidable heat.

"But this time I get out there and, by God, there's smoke rolling out of the chimney. Somebody had gotten themselves dedicated to that squalid little cabin. So being the snoop that I am, I start tiptoeing up to the front door to see if I could get a peek at whoever had taken up residence. I was about a quarter step up the porch when I hear, chikchik. Yep. Sonofabitch had racked his shotgun. Whoever was inside was ready to have themselves a shootout and it didn't take me any time to slink off the way I'd come. Can't say who it was, but I'm guessing they aren't up to any good. Thought you might be interested."

"Ferlin?"

"Yeah?"

"Can you lead us back there?"

"Sure thing. Whenever you'd like."

"How about now? I think right now would be best."

Ferlin led the way in his maroon Jeep followed by Wilson and then Shef in their black and whites. The road was gravelly and wracked with potholes. Jack firs and young alders crowded the way and slapped against their windows as they drove on and on into a lonely, unloved hinterland. Eventually they came to a wide circular dead end and all three parked and stepped out of their vehicles.

Above the canopy a gray pall was still smothering the sky. Sunshine seemed but a rumor, and neither did cheery birdsong grace that quarter. Perhaps a whiff of pesticides hung in the air. Only a raven croaked as it flew overhead, its wingbeats plainly heard in the uncanny quiet.

"How far away is it from here?" Wilson asked.

"Hard to say," said Ferlin. "Maybe a mile and a half."

"Could we find the place on our own?"

"If you had about a week."

"Let us lead then. I don't want you getting yourself into trouble."

"What do you think this is for?" Ferlin said, revealing the huge pistol at his hip.

"I appreciate the sentiment. We'll lead."

On they went by foot. First along a fading deer trail, then atop the bank of a swift, roiling creek. It was an old second-growth forest they traversed, soon to be logged off and burned, soon to earn its keep. In the distance, they could hear a woodpecker hammering after a meal and some chipmunks spotted them and cried of trespass. Mushrooms both benign and poisonous grew in clumps about the floor. Wilson finally stopped and checked his watch. Shef and Ferlin drew in close.

"How much farther?" Wilson asked.

"Not far," Ferlin said. He squatted down and began drawing a map in the dirt with his forefinger. "It's just back around on the other side of this rise. Down into a little draw where two creeks run together is where the cabin sits. Quarter mile or so."

"Then I want you to stay right here. If you hear gunfire, run back and call for assistance. I need you to do that for me."

"You sure you wouldn't rather me come along?"

"I can't let you."

Ferlin smiled. "I was kind of hoping you'd say that."

"Give us about an hour before you start worrying about us. Just hang tight."

Wilson and Shef brandished their guns and went up and around the slope until they could no longer see Ferlin. They began to pick their steps carefully, eyes attuned to movement of any sort. Wilson looked back to see how Shef was doing and the golden boy nodded and tried to conceal a mounting trepidation. Something beyond him snagged Wilson's attention. A crouching mass of fur, obscured by a dense thicket. Wilson squinted for a better view.

"What?" Shef said.

"I don't know. I see something."

Shef turned and they looked together. The fur shifted and two eyeballs appeared. A nose. Maybe a tongue. Some shaggy brown humanoid was staring directly at them.

"What is that?" Shef asked.

"I don't know."

Shef's voice began to sound panicky. "Look at it. Tom. It looks just like—"

"Quiet."

"Oh fuck. Oh my God. Ferlin was right. This place *is* inhabited. It's Bigfoot. Right there. Fucking Bigfoot."

"Stop talking."

"I'm done. I'm going back to the city."

There was a low grunt and the creature rose up hugely to two legs. Shef appeared ready to shoot and Wilson rested his hand on his forearm to calm him as the beast dropped and ran off on all fours. There was some crashing of foliage and then only the quiet of the forest.

"Take it easy," Wilson said. "It was just a cinnamon black bear."

Shef lowered his gun and bent over with his hands on his knees. "Just a bear. Never thought those words would be used to calm me down."

"Come on. We've got to keep moving."

"Fuck me. Ain't this a way to be going after some maniac in the deep dark woods."

"You scared?"

"Hell yeah, I'm scared."

"Good. If the hair on the back of your neck isn't standing straight up, then there's something wrong with you."

Wilson moved to lead them onward.

"Tom?"

"Yeah?"

"I've never shot at anybody before."

"Well, neither have I. If we do this properly, we can keep it that way."

They went on over the rise and it wasn't long before they could see the cabin down in the draw as Ferlin had explained. When they were within a hundred yards they stopped and scouted from behind an old cedar nurse log.

The cabin looked surprisingly cozy, nestled as it was amongst the mossy trees and the white flowing waters. There was a woodshed and a small footbridge and a dilapidated hitching post. A place where a hermit might just eke out a raw existence.

"So what's our plan?" Shef asked.

"We'll sneak in from the left side where there's some good cover. If we haven't been made yet then we'll run up between the door and the window and holler that it's time to come out."

"What if he loads that shotgun again and holes himself up inside?"

"Then we smoke him out."

"We're gonna set fire to the cabin?"

"No. But we're gonna say that we are. And we're going to sound very convincing. Why do you think I brought this gas can?"

Wilson held his arm out, hefting the imaginary receptacle. Shef grinned and they began to creep along until they were within twenty yards. Nothing had stirred.

"Change of plans," Wilson whispered. "If we get up onto the porch and haven't heard anything then I'm kicking in that door. You give me backup. We'll go on three."

"I'm not in love with your new plan."

"Neither am I. Let's get on with it."

Guns out, they made it briskly to the porch. Wilson took the first groaning step. Another. And one more. He seemed to glide the last six feet and then was at the door. Wilson held up one finger. Two. Three and he had launched his boot at the door which splintered and flung open to reveal a man in bed just jolting out of an afternoon nap. A large and leery fellow. Griz.

"Freeze," Wilson screamed. "Do not move or I will light your ass up."

Griz remained resting on one elbow, his eyes going back and forth between Wilson and Shef and their weapons.

"Who else is here with you?" Wilson asked.

"It's just me," Griz said, his voice sounding even more raspy and languid than usual.

"There better not be any surprises."

"It's just me."

Wilson directed Shef to clear the cabin while he kept his pistol aimed squarely on Griz's chest.

"Ain't you gonna show me your warrant?" Griz asked.

Wilson only stared at him.

"You ain't gonna be able to hold me unless you got a warrant."

"That right?"

"You don't seem to know much law for a lawman."

In a minute Shef returned. "Cabin's all clear. There's some drug paraphernalia lying around the place. I assume he's got a stash hidden somewhere."

"Did you spot the shotgun?"

"No."

"Where's the gun?" Wilson asked him.

"Wouldn't you like to know."

"Get out of that bed. Keep your hands where I can see them."

Griz slowly tossed the covers from himself, swung his legs to the floor, and stood with his palms up and facing outward. He seemed to be finding something very humorous.

"Now go put your hands against that wall and stay there until I tell you otherwise."

"I've got rights, you know."

"Against the wall."

Griz looked them over brazenly as if there might be some weakness he could exploit.

"Do it. Now."

Taking his sweet time, Griz finally turned and put his hands against the wall.

"Cover me," Wilson said. "If he so much as twitches, you blast away."

Shef nodded and kept his gun poised and Wilson moved forward until he was only a few feet behind Griz. Then he knelt down and peered under the bed. The shotgun lay among a swarm of cobwebs and pellets of mouse shit. He stood and checked to see if the weapon was loaded. It was. He held it out before him.

"Turn around," Wilson said.

As Griz was turning, he said, "Ain't you gonna read me——"

Wilson had swung the butt of the shotgun around like a club and cracked him a tremendous echoing blow aside the skull. Griz's eyes rolled back like marbles and he went stumbling into a shelf spilling paperbacks and nudie magazines. As he was struggling to recover, Wilson casually stepped forward and rammed the stock into Griz's gut. Griz wheezed and doubled over, and as his head dropped, Wilson snapped his chin back with a swift uppercut. Griz fell against the wall and crumpled to the ground, moaning and dribbling blood from his mouth.

Shef was beside himself. "Tom! What the hell are you doing?"

"Fucking pigs," Griz gurgled.

Wilson tossed the shotgun to the bed and flew upon Griz's chest like some outlandish eagle. His first fist was deflected, but his second smashed into Griz's nose with an awful crunch of cartilage. Another swipe opened up a gash under Griz's right eye, and the flowing blood seemed to goad Wilson into greater savagery, blow after blow hailing down like a true tempest of wrath. Griz was cursing and struggling and shielding his face the best he could, but Wilson was lost to vengeance, battering away at that body in a brainless fury. Griz began to go limp, his face mangled as ground beef. Wilson would have kept on but he finally felt himself being tugged backward to his feet. In unconscious reflex Wilson wheeled around to confront this new assailant as Shef waved his hands out in front of him.

"It's me. It's me."

Wilson stood there panting as he slowly regained himself. Blood speckled his face and Shef stared at him in horror.

"Christ, Tom. Look at what you've done."

Wilson gazed down upon Griz's ragged, lifeless form.

"Look at him. He might be dead."

W ilson shuffled into the sergeant's office holding his splinted wrist up close to his chest. Two broken fingers had been taped together and small bandages clung to his neck and cheek. Sergeant Davies appeared too furious to look at him as he scrawled a brief memo. Wilson sat and waited for what may come.

When the sergeant was finished, he slammed his pen atop the desk and looked up in a simmering rage. "What the hell happened to you out there?"

"He resisted."

"Bullshit. You lost your mind. What you did was insane. I'm looking at these pictures and I can see no difference between what you did to Griz and what he did to that security guard eight years ago. No difference whatsoever. You damn near killed him."

"He deserves it."

"Maybe he does deserve it. But that's not how we administer justice around here. You acted like a goddamn vigilante, not a Clark County deputy sheriff."

"I got him though. That ought to count for something."

"Sure. We'll pop him on a few charges. But thanks to you, the DA is mulling over a deal to drop the charges so the county won't get sued."

Wilson scratched at an itch underneath his splint.

"I know exactly why you wailed on him out there. You still think he had something to do with the shooting. That's it, isn't it?"

Wilson nodded slowly.

"See. See this is where if you'd acted like a professional deputy instead of some benighted lunatic you wouldn't be up shit creek without a paddle. Because you're dead wrong."

"What do you mean?"

"We kept telling you that Griz had an alibi. You kept saying there was no proof. And you'd been right about that. Until today. While you were in the hospital getting your battle wounds mended, I was here on the phone chatting with Detective Depp. He managed to track down a receptionist in Chico, California, who is willing to testify that she checked Griz into her motel the night of the shooting. So there you have it. Your hunch was off. We already have the perpetrator in custody just like we'd been trying to tell you."

Wilson felt his whole spirit sag and the consequences of what he'd done began to hit home and drag him even further.

"You're going to be put on an indefinite leave of absence," the sergeant announced. "Officially we'll be attributing this episode to severe emotional strain. I'd suggest you call your guild rep the first chance you get."

There seemed to be nothing more to say and Wilson began to rise.

"Hold it." The sergeant pushed a stack of files aside so he could lean forward and rest his elbows on the desk. "I'm worried about you, Tom. I'm worried about how far you might keep sliding."

"Sarge, I—"

"Just keep your trap shut until I've finished saying my piece."

Wilson sat back in his chair as the sergeant took a moment to collect his words.

"When I was still pretty young as a cop I got called to a house fire in Vancouver. Me and my partner got there before the firefighters did. Inside, a couple of white trash idiots were still lying on the couch, passed out and drunk. We woke them up and told them what was happening and they started shrieking about their kids. We ran upstairs where the fire was really working and had to turn back for the heat. The firefighters finally got there and put down the flames and then we were able to get to the kids.

"There were five of them, all in their beds. Having a big sleepover. I carried one of the boys out of there in my arms. He was charred all over, and as I was carrying him out his skin started coming off on me. It was horrible. Afterwards, we laid all the kids down in the grass. The parents were out of their minds and we had to drag them away. One little girl survived. That's it.

"The worst thing about it all was the smell. It was like meat on a barbeque and I had the smell in my clothes, my hair. It still makes me sick to think about it. I don't believe I was able to eat a hot dog or a sausage for about a year and half. And I loved eating that stuff.

"After that I spiraled. I wouldn't talk about it with my wife. In fact, at that time we were specifically told not to talk about it with our wives, not to burden them with those kinds of stories. And instead of dealing with the emotional trauma of it all, I took to drinking to cope. Like most of us did then. I got out of control and my wife finally told me enough was enough and she took the kids with her and never came home."

The sergeant leaned back and watched Wilson until he would look at him.

"That's what can happen if you don't deal with your head like you need to. I see how you are now and I know you need help. You're about one little thing away from a total meltdown. And that would be a true shame because you're an excellent deputy. You might even make an excellent sergeant one day if you can get through this. So take some time to get your head right. Go be with your wife and see your new kid born. When is Ellen due again?"

"Any day now."

"Then don't miss that. This'll all still be here when you're ready."

IV

Statement by Dean Matsu
Olympia, Washington
June 1982, 2 years after eruption

When the volcano started erupting again in May I told myself that I was done climbing it. I'd already made it to the crater a half dozen times and I figured that I'd probably used up all my good luck. Well that lasted for a couple weeks and then I decided that I had to have one last go. I was really a zealot about climbing then. I took a lot of chances.

It was very early on the seventeenth when I ran into him on the mountain. I was going down and he was coming up. It was still several hours until dawn as you had to make the summit and get back down below timberline before light or else the authorities might see you. Well, as I was coming down I was glissading through this little chute when all of a sudden I looked over and saw this guy trudging up the scree about twenty yards away. It surprised the hell out of me. I thought I was hallucinating for a second. I hadn't seen anyone else that far up since the eruptions started. So I dug my axe in and got myself stopped and he walked over.

Right away I could tell that he wasn't any great mountaineer. His gear was pretty ratty and he was really huffing and puffing and exhausted looking. He asked me how much longer it would take him to reach the summit and I told him he had about another two hours. He seemed pretty disheartened that he wasn't closer. I warned him that he'd better hurry up or he wasn't going to make it back down before dawn, but he said that didn't concern him. I told him the authorities would slap him with a big fine if they caught him, but he didn't seem worried about that either. He said all he cared about was having a look into the crater. And then he started right back up the mountain.

I watched him for a bit and then called out to him asking what his name was. I don't know why I did that exactly. Guess he seemed like someone worth remembering. He paused and thought about it for a moment and said, oh you'll probably know my name soon enough. And before I could reply he started back up toward the crater. So I let him be.

The rest of the way down I kept wondering what he could have meant by that. It seemed like such an odd answer. When I finally made it to timberline I looked back up the mountain and I thought I could see him moving like a little speck of silhouette on the rim of the crater. And that's when it occurred to me that he might be planning on throwing himself into it. Like some self-sacrifice thing. All day I kept dwelling on it. Imaging different scenarios. Then when the mountain blew the next morning I figured that if he hadn't thrown himself in, he'd probably been blown to pieces. So I was surprised when neither of those things turned out to be the case. And I was especially surprised when I learned what the true story was.

Now, I know a lot of people have said that he must have been crazy or evil for doing what he did. But I'm not so sure that he was either of those things. He was confused is what he was. The whole situation was very sad and he got twisted up inside of it all. Maybe I shouldn't be saying this but I think I understand him to some degree. I'm not saying that I condone what he did. But I don't think he's evil. I think it's laziness to dismiss him like that. I'd even go so far as to say that oftentimes what people consider evil is just something they can't really comprehend. Or don't want to.

Wilson stood outside the hospital cafeteria waiting for breakfast to be served. Dawn was just arriving and he watched the patio garden grow vivid through incremental hues and then suddenly flare golden as the infant sun fought its way through the trees. Wilson was reflecting on fortune's tide when a cafeteria worker unlocked the door and called out that the food was ready.

Along with a few other visitors, Wilson went and grabbed a plastic tray and slid it along the metal rails of the sneeze guard as a matronly attendant scooped this and that breakfast item onto a pair of plates. When he'd reached the end of the line the woman asked him if he cared for anything to drink.

"A carton of milk," he said. "And two orange juices. And a large coffee."

The cashier rang him up and Wilson carried the tray back to the elevator and took it to their room on the second floor. He elbowed open the door as quietly as he could and Ellen's parents stirred in their chairs but settled again and continued dozing.

From the hospital bed Ellen smiled at him like some disheveled angel, tired and scruffy and glowing with the bliss of fresh motherhood. On her chest rested their newborn boy, taking in his tiny first breaths as she gently caressed his head. Wilson approached holding the tray.

"What did you get?" she asked quietly.

"Everything. What would you like?"

"I don't know. Just come over and sit with me for a minute."

Wilson set the tray down on the table and took a seat at the edge of the bed.

"I'm so proud of you," he said. "You did so good."

"And I'm so happy you could be here this time."

"So am I. It was the second greatest moment of my life."

"What was the first?"

"When you said that you'd marry me."

They shared a long intimate look and then he leaned in to give her a kiss, her lips tasting of sweat. Afterwards he stroked her hair and together they gazed in astonishment at their incredible mewling creation.

"What should we name him?" she asked.

"I don't know."

"I was thinking we could name him Lesley if you want."

"No. I don't want that."

"Well. What does he look like his name should be?"

Wilson stared at the boy. "He looks kind of like a frog at this point. How about Kermit?"

"That's about the last name I would ever choose."

"What about Toad then?"

"Toad Wilson. Now that one's got a ring to it."

They both laughed aloud as Ellen's mother harrumphed and babbled some dreamy gibberish. Ellen held a finger to her lips and they spoke more softly.

"I'm so glad that it's all over finally," she said.

"The pregnancy?"

"No. You know. . ."

"Ah."

"I'm sorry that it turned out to be Elmer, but at least it's done with. They got him. *You* got him. You should feel proud."

"Yeah, well . . . I'm just sorry I was so hard to live with there for a while. You deserve a merit badge for putting up with me the way you did."

"It wasn't so bad."

Wilson lifted an eyebrow.

"Well . . . Yeah, it was pretty hard. But I'm tough. I'm tough enough to handle you."

"We make a good team."

"We make a great team."

Wilson glanced at the plastic tray. "You know, your breakfast is sitting here getting cold. Are you hungry?"

"I could probably eat something."

"Very well, my lady," Wilson said in an atrocious imitation of an English butler. He turned and took up the tray. "Let's see what delectable items we have here. Ah ha. For breakfast this morning you have the choice of our finest rubber eggs, not one but two pieces of dreadfully nutritious toast, some greasy pork thingies, greasy fried potato pucks, fruit salad . . . actually that one looks pretty good . . . and finally, madam, let's not overlook it, one bowl of drool. Gruel. I mean, oatmeal."

Ellen was already giggling mightily and it required great effort to remain quiet as he guided her through the selection of beverages. When he'd arranged her plate the way she liked it, he went around the bed to check on Maggie, the little girl still slumbering soundly on a miniature cot.

After they'd both eaten, Ellen's eyelids showed their heaviness and Wilson encouraged her to sleep. She nodded and he tucked her into the covers.

"I'm very happy," he said.

"And I'm very happy that you're happy."

"Get some rest now."

"Okay."

Once she'd faded off, Wilson gathered up the remains of their breakfast and took it back down to the cafeteria. He thought he might go out to smoke one of his celebratory cigars but instead he took the elevator up to the third floor where the guard was stationed as always outside Louanne's door.

"Hey there, Hank," Wilson said.

"Hey yourself. Congratulations."

"Mind if I pop in and say hello?"

"Don't see why not. Heck, maybe today's the day."

"Maybe."

Hank rose and unlocked the door.

Wilson stepped inside and then turned and asked, "Say, how much longer are they going to keep you guys posted here?"

"Won't be much longer now that they've got the guy in custody. We'll probably fart around here for another week or so and then it's back to the real world."

"I see. Well, I'll just be a few minutes."

"Take as long as you'd like."

The door shut and locked and Wilson stepped toward the bed. Louanne lay exactly as she had the previous times but her wounds had healed enough that she no longer wore any bandages. These days Wilson was able to look at her without torment. Now it was mostly a comfort to be in her presence, to know that she was still alive.

He walked over to the window and drew the blinds wide open and a deluge of sunlight filled the room and washed over Louanne so that she appeared like some celestial sleeper. He pulled out a chair and sat beside her bed.

There were so many things he wanted to share with her, and though it may have been in vain he went on and explained what had become of the world while she'd been away. He told her about the mountain and the ash and the earthquakes. He told her about Harry Truman. He explained what had happened in Iran and about the Trojan nuclear plant. Lastly, he told her that Ellen had just given birth to a healthy boy, and as he did so he watched her closely to see if maybe she'd react in some very subtle way. She did not. She only lay there peacefully as always, lost in some inexplicable otherworld.

When he was finished, he stood and closed the blinds. Then he turned to tell Louanne goodbye and he froze there disbelieving his eyes for it seemed that she had shifted. He moved to the edge of her bed and time crawled as he waited for something more. He'd nearly given it up when she seemed to whimper. Wilson looked around the room as though there might be someone else to verify this and then leaned in close, closer, his ear to her very lips. Again he waited, and finally he heard her murmur a single word, the breath of a dream.

"Wake up," he implored.

But she would only continue sleeping.

T heir once flourishing property now appeared desolate, imbued with ruin. All the animals had been herded off and sold. The grass had grown to a scraggly length and the weeds were beginning to take hold. The house itself did look haunted, so dark and forlorn were the windows to its lifeless interior. Around the premises, police tape cordoned off the official crime scene, and Wilson pulled up to a yellow ribbon that sagged between two trees like some lonely old swing.

He got out of his truck, stepped over the tape, and walked up to the front door. It was locked. Next he tried the door to the pantry and then the one on the back porch and they too were locked. He began going from window to window until he found one that slid open. It was a tight squeeze but he managed to get through feet first and landed with a thump in the bathtub.

He went down the hall, toward where he had found them reposed in their own blood. He stopped. He would not revisit that room unless it was necessary. What he was looking for was Louanne's address book and he found it next to the telephone. He flipped through the pages, paused, and dialed the number. There were several rings and finally a croaking female voice said hello.

"This is Deputy Wilson with the Clark County Sheriff's Department. Is this Patricia Clark?"

"Yes."

"I'm sorry to bother you so early in the morning but I'm trying to get in touch with your son. We've been acquaintances here in Washington."

"What's this about? Is he in trouble?"

"I just need to chat with him. The last time we spoke he said he was moving back to California. Is he there now?"

"He came to visit me and then he left again."

"Do you know where he might be?"

"He said he was going to spend some time at his grandparents' cabin."

"On Spirit Lake?"

"Yeah."

"That cabin is in the restricted zone."

"I know it. I told him that. He went anyway."

"Alright. Thank you very much."

"Deputy?"

"Yes, ma'am?"

"Will you see if you can get him to come down from there? I'm worried that something might happen to him."

"I'll see what I can do."

"And Deputy?"

"Yes?"

"He's not in his right mind. I think you should know that."

Wilson hung up the phone and gazed at the calendar on the wall. It still read April, the dates filled with appointments neither of them had kept. He flipped the page, left it on May, and then went searching for the documents to the cabin.

S pirit Lake Highway was already packed with sightseers on that fair-weathered Saturday, so many people aspiring to history and cataclysm from a safe distance. Progress was slow through Toutle, and Wilson banged on his wheel and disparaged the masses of confused tourists. In the high school parking lot, he noticed a large gathering of vehicles, which included news vans and several Skamania County sheriff's cars. Beyond the town, the highway opened and he put his foot to the gas.

He was but a few turns from the roadblock when he suddenly stopped and pulled into a turnout. Parked there was Doug's yellow Jeep. Wilson got out and looked toward the mountain, estimating the distance to the cabin. It was not close and he drove on.

When he arrived at the roadblock, a National Guardsman came over in his grungy outsized helmet and tried to send him away. Wilson showed the property tax forms.

"You must have missed the memo," the guardsman said, shifting the rifle slung over his shoulder. "You're all supposed to gather at the school in Toutle. We'll be letting you through in about an hour."

"Can't you just let me slip in since I'm already here? I am a cabin owner."

"I don't care if you're Magic Johnson. The only way you're getting through is if you're in that convoy."

Wilson drove back to the school and walked around waiting for noon to arrive. The cabin owners were obvious enough, nearly all of them wearing baby blue shirts with an outline of the mountain and the words, *I own a piece of the rock*. Mostly they mingled about eating doughnuts and swapping stories with neighbors. Wilson didn't want to attract any attention so he kept his head down and merely eavesdropped. At the outskirts of the group he stopped to listen to one of the more vocal owners who'd been delighting a reporter with his righteous indignation.

"If there's a risk in living up there then it oughta be our right as property owners to take it," said a defiant man in a cowboy hat. "How would you like it if someone came up to you and said that you couldn't live in your home anymore because of what some fancy pants scientists are saying? Well it might. It might just do that, but it also might not. And that's our gamble to take. Besides that, there's a big two-headed snake on the loose out here. Yessir. I said, two-headed. Well, sure. It's that they're forbidding us regular folks from accessing our properties and yet they're allowing Harry Truman to stay up there in his lodge. How's that for a double standard? For some reason the authorities are treating Harry Truman just like he's a god. Yep. You heard me right. And furthermore, I think . . ."

Wilson felt a tap on his shoulder and he turned to see a Skamania County deputy.

"Are you one of the homeowners?" the deputy asked.

"I am."

"Can I see some proof of ownership?"

Wilson hesitated and then passed him the documents.

The deputy looked them over. "Lesley Jenkins?"

"That's right."

"Hmm. That's a familiar—"

"Is there something I need to sign here?"

"Right." The deputy passed him back the documents along with a clipboard and a stack of waivers. "Print your name there. Sign and date there. You can read through the form if you'd like, but what it boils down to is that you're absolving the state and county agencies of any responsibility for your well-being while you're inside the restricted area. It says that you're aware of the risks and you're taking them anyway, yadda yadda."

"How long will we get?"

"Until dusk."

Noon came and the Skamania County sheriff gave a brief announcement about the expected protocol and then began to lead the convoy up the road to Spirit Lake. Wilson was close to the rear of the file, and after he and a few more homeowners passed through the roadblock, several National Guardsmen began to seal the barricade once again. Overhead, a

Washington State Patrol plane circled the area, ready to radio a warning should the mountain show any worrisome activity.

Near Spirit Lake, homeowners began to scatter off to clear out valuables and feed stranded pets, and Wilson drove on to the Jenkins' cabin. The landscape around the property was ghastly compared to the month before. A fine layer of ash now covered everything and the grass was slowly being smothered. Alder trees had yet to bud out, and in their naked lankiness they looked like the last survivors of some merciless siege. Wilson took the short path to the cabin and as he stepped up onto the porch he saw that the boards were beginning to slump under a heavy blanket of ash which had been disturbed by boot tracks amounting to perhaps a dozen comings and goings.

Even now he had no plan, no evidence. Nothing but a single word from a senile woman and his own hazy, half-formed suspicions. He turned to appraise the mountain. It was calm, silent, and misshapen from the pressure within. No one should have been that close. Even the air seemed somehow dense with dread.

Wilson approached the cabin door. His hand went to his armpit where a pistol was concealed beneath his jacket, but he decided to leave it where it was. He knocked, waited, knocked again. Then he twisted the knob and cautiously pushed open the door.

"Hello . . . Anybody here? Doug? Anybody?"

He stepped inside the dark shuttered cabin that he and Lesley had stripped to a Spartan austerity. The dining table and chairs remained. The couch, the stove, a pile of wood, and not much else. Wilson began to climb the hand-hewn stairs calling Doug's name. Again his hand went to his gun and again he left it holstered.

The loft was vacant, but it was apparent that Doug had been hiding there. Several bedframes lined the walls of the cramped and pitched space, and atop the last bed lay a sleeping bag and a makeshift pillow comprised of Doug's spare shirts. Along the floor of the bed huddled a small legion of empty pint bottles, as well as a pipe, a tattered Louie L'Amour novel, some toiletries and food wrappers. And lastly a small black journal.

Wilson bent and picked up the moleskin diary. He turned it over in his hand and rubbed the leather binding, slightly superstitious about such an invasion of privacy. Finally, he sat on the bed and opened to a random page. *Today I officially quit drinking*, read an entry in neat blocky handwriting. Wilson leafed through the pages, the legibility varying dramatically from one entry to the next, alcohol an obvious detriment to his penmanship. *Fuck that fucking cunt*, began a sloppy diatribe about his ex-wife. Wilson began to slow down and peruse each page as the passages became more abstract and disturbing. He flipped the page and read the next entry which was but a single line.

Nightmares. Nightmares. Please God. Show me mercy as I showed them.

T he tourists had mostly all gone home by this blackened hour, and Toutle was again a town of quiet and somnolent obscurity. Wilson stood outside the gas station smoking a cigarette and drinking another cup of coffee to ward off his sleepless fatigue. At dusk, he and all the other homeowners had been rounded up by the sheriff and forced to leave with the convoy. Doug had not returned.

He could go back tomorrow. He had already signed up. So many homeowners had shown interest in returning to their cabins that another caravan was scheduled to leave at ten the next morning. He thought about Ellen, for whom he had left only a vague note. Vaguer intentions dizzied his weary mind and he felt as though he were way out on the edge of something that may topple at any instant.

Tomorrow. He could go back tomorrow. Wilson tossed his cigarette to the pavement and stubbed it out with his boot. He swallowed the last of his coffee and took it inside to refill once more. Then he climbed into his truck and drove back up the highway toward Spirit Lake and the cabin and the volcano that was loaded like the gun he wore against his ribs.

The cabin was too far from Doug's Jeep for hiking at that hour so

Wilson instead began scouting out the logging roads that some were still using to sneak around the official roadblock. After encountering several locked gates, he eventually found an open road, and as it split and split again he sometimes took his bearing by a compass, but more often by the moonwashed mountain itself. All along the way the road was flanked by acre after acre of trashy clearcuts. The forest slashed to stumps and vanishing these past weeks in an ever more urgent haste to rip out the timber before Mount St. Helens did.

Wilson drove on into a dead end. Then another. Finally, he'd exhausted all the most likely roads to Spirit Lake, and after a long private debate he resolved to complete the last uncertain expanse by foot.

He locked the truck and then set off toward the mountain with only his meek flashlight to lead the way. He took a few steps and then stopped and looked up as if the heavens might bestow some final courage or approval. Mute as always, the stars only winked in their customary perches. Nearby an owl hooted once, then twice. Wilson spotted the bird atop a fir tree and the owl bobbed its head around like a boxer in the limelight and then took off screeching through the night.

Once inside the canopy of the forest, the sky was erased and blackness reigned. Of all the darkness he'd grown accustomed to, this place was the darkest yet. Everything beyond his small light was like the depths of the ocean to a nightfaring mariner and he would not even allow himself to consider what might happen should his light fail. He fought through an aggression of brambles and then past some spindly trees that clawed at him like witches. Footsteps of anonymous creatures were scurrying hither and thither and he happened into some sticky arachnid's web. Legs scrabbled across his neck and he lurched and swiped at himself and cursed aloud, his voice echoing falsetto down a corridor of trees. He paused and shined the light around him in a full circle as if to cauterize his fear and then continued once more.

The simplest way to keep going was to walk quickly and concentrate on something else. His mind chose Lesley, that great friend grinning so vividly wherever such images are stored for safe keeping. He would understand why Wilson was here. He would not be happy, but he would understand. *They always told me to leave my work at the station, he had once said. But I often thought that was an excuse for not really giving a damn.* And with such memories, Wilson finally pushed through a mass of branches and walked out into a large open glade.

He didn't know where he was until he went down toward the lake and saw the spacious lodge hunkered against the edge of the forest. Harry Truman's abode. Beyond this, the mountain loomed over the timberline, etched by the moon into colossal silhouette. Wilson went on through the clearing, hoping to pick up the road to the cabin. He was striding along the side of the lodge when a gruff voice accosted him from the porch shadows.

"Who goes there?" Truman demanded.

Wilson stopped and peered and finally saw the old man just beginning to rise from a lawn chair.

"Sorry to disturb you, Harry. I'm just trying to get over to the Jenkins' cabin."

"You some kind of a nitwit? Spooking around at night like this. What right you got to be at that cabin?"

"I've been a close friend of the family. My name's Tom Wilson and I'm a Clark County deputy sheriff."

"Okay, but that don't answer my question."

"I'm here to speak with their grandson."

"What the hell you got to talk to him about that's cause for sneaking out here like a goddamn imbecile?"

"It's a long story."

"Does it look like I'm pressed for time?"

"I'm sorry, Harry. I've really got to get out to see him."

"Boy, get your ass up on this porch and start making some sense. Otherwise I'm gonna call up the authorities first thing and tell them they've got a renegade deputy out here named Tom Wilson stirring up some trouble."

Wilson shifted with impatience. "You'd do that?"

"Goddamn right I would."

Wilson knew that the old man was probably just in need of company, but he also knew that he wasn't the type to make an empty threat so he reluctantly stepped up onto the porch. A cat crept over and rubbed its head against Wilson's shin as Truman slurped at his Schenley's and Coke, the eighty-three-year-old man a rosy-cheeked curmudgeon and thoroughly creased with wrinkles.

"Is this grandson the one that's been coming over here pestering me most every day?" Truman asked.

"I don't know. What's he look like?"

"He looks like a feather-brained drunk. Dagnabbed hair gelled up like some city slicking sleezeball. Came over here the other night asking me if he could borrow an axe. I said, it's dark out. You're gonna cut yourself down to the damn nubs, and besides that there's not even supposed to be anybody out here except for me. He started in with some cockamamie excuses and I flat told him to bugger off. I don't like the look of him. What do you think? He sound like the grandson you're looking for?"

"Yeah. That's him."

Truman shook his head sadly. "Lesley and Louanne were some outstanding folk. That was a real tragedy what happened to them. A true sobber. He's really their grandson?"

"Hard to believe, huh?"

"They say the apple don't fall far from the tree, but I guess it must sometimes get rolling down a hill or something cause that apple wound up about a mile or two away."

Wilson began to shuffle backwards. "Harry, I really need to get going."

"Hey now. You ain't upheld your part of the bargain yet."

"If I'm right about why I'm up here, then you'll know all about it soon enough."

"That ain't at all satisfying to me."

"I'm sorry, but it'll have to do for now."

Wilson stepped down off the porch, took some strides through the yard, and then turned. "Are you still planning on staying up here and seeing this thing through?"

"I'm not going anywhere," Truman replied.

"What'll you do if she blows?"

"I'll sit right here and watch it."

Wilson nodded, gave the old man a salute, and continued down the road.

The Jenkins' cabin was exactly as it had been at dusk. Wilson made a quick scan of the loft just to be sure and then he went outside to the end of the dock.

Spirit Lake looked like a tremendous spill of ink and on its rippling surface the stars skittered about like lightning bugs. Small waves gurgled against the canoe and lapped at the shore and in the shallows the frogs were singing their riotous music. Wilson watched a bat swoop and squeak and disappear and then his eyes roamed farther as he began to follow the ridgeline of the volcano up to its bulging apex. He tried to fathom the incredible forces roiling beneath him at that moment, but in his wearied state it all seemed too massive, too imponderable. All he knew for sure was that there was absolutely nothing that could be relied upon anymore. Not rocks and stones. Not mountains. Not even the earth itself.

After a long while, Wilson finally walked back to the cabin. He took a seat in the corner of the room and waited for Doug to return.

I n his exhaustion Wilson had fallen asleep, and he was drooling like a dog on the shoulder of his jacket when the creak of the cabin door awoke him. He lifted his head and blinked his eyes open as Doug trudged in from the blue morning and shut the door behind him. Doug dropped his pack to the floor, stomped the soil from his boots, and then started off toward the stairs.

"Enjoy your hike?" Wilson asked.

Doug halted midstride. "Tom? What are you doing here?"

"Why don't you tell me."

"What do you mean?"

Wilson stood up from the chair. "You shot them, didn't you?"

"What?"

"You shot your grandparents, didn't you?"

"That's crazy. How could you even think that?"

"Show me mercy as I showed them."

"You read my journal? That's fucked up, dude. And you're off your rocker if that's what you think I meant by that."

"Oh yeah?"

"You think I'm a murderer? You think I'd shoot my own grandparents?"

"I think it's time we take a walk."

"To where?"

"To my truck. So I can take you to see the detective."

"This whole thing's warped your brain. They've already got Elmer in custody."

"Time to go."

"I'm not going anywhere."

Wilson opened his jacket and removed his gun. "Time to go."

"You'd shoot me?"

"Only if you try to run."

"Fuck you. You're crazy."

"Maybe. Doesn't mean I'm wrong though."

"They're gonna fire your ass."

"Not if I'm right they won't."

"I can't believe this. I thought we were like family."

"Les and Louanne were family to me. I never thought you were more than a derelict."

Doug made a bitter face and waved his arm in the air. "Fine then. Let's go. I'm already looking forward to when they take your badge from you."

They exited the cabin and started along the bright sunlit road. Doug led while Wilson followed a few paces behind with his pistol swinging in his right hand. Fir trees scented their progress and already the cool air was beginning to warm. Altogether it was a most idyllic morning. Yet for some reason the birds were not singing.

Soon they passed along Harry Truman's lodge. The old codger did not show and they carried on. At the forest's edge, Doug finally stopped to plead with his captor.

"Tom, this is ridiculous. Put the gun away and let's talk this out."

Wilson cocked the hammer and leveled the pistol with greater menace.

"Look at you. You're confused. You don't even know what you're doing anymore. Let's just stop here for a minute and have a chat."

"Keep moving."

"Which way are we even headed?"

"Straight on through the trees there. I'll let you know if you're going the wrong direction."

Doug shook his head and they went on into the woods. The path that had seemed like such a terror the night before was now a charming stroll. With the advantage of daylight it took but thirty minutes to reach Wilson's truck. At first Doug would not get inside the vehicle, but after some brute persuasion he finally climbed in the cab wordlessly like a demoralized prisoner of war. Wilson started up the truck and began making the turns back toward the highway.

Several miles along he slowed to a stop. An alder tree had fallen across the road and would need to be cleared away.

"I suppose you're gonna make me drag that off the road," Doug said.

"Now you're getting it."

Wilson stood a few yards back as Doug tugged the young alder into the roadside ditch. They were just returning to the truck when Doug paused and aimed his ear at the mountain which was hidden somewhere beyond the trees.

"What's that sound?" Doug asked.

"Stop stalling and get in the truck."

"Seriously. Listen to that."

It began as any shush of wind, and Wilson began to take interest as the noise rapidly grew into what sounded like innumerable pellets being fired through the forest. Overhead, the crowns of the trees were bending and snapping, and above that the scant white clouds were turning crimson and gray. Then the forest was all rumble and roar.

They had finally begun to run for the truck when a hot black raging smog swept them up like puny ragdolls and body-slammed them into the road. Wilson hit chest-first with such an impact that his lungs caved. The cracks he heard seemed to be his ribs, but were in fact the firs crashing around him. He was gasping for oxygen when a tree fell upon his legs to vise him to the hostile earth. Next a scalding brew of mud and ash began to cover him and boil his flesh. He felt his ears stiffen and curl. So hot was the slurry that he could only imagine it was lava. Choking and burning and pinned to the ground, Wilson waited for his life to end as missiles of rock and glacial ice detonated around him in that alpine apocalypse. Somehow he hadn't even heard the mountain explode.

Death must sometimes play coy, for Wilson was finally able to filter a few breaths from the ash-dense air that coated his mouth like talcum powder. With excruciating effort, he managed to lift himself up to his elbows and twist enough to see the tree that pinned him down. He struggled, but he could do nothing to make the tree budge. His legs may have been shattered. He wasn't sure. His gun had blown off somewhere and his skin was roasting beneath a foot of fiery ash. Below him the ground shuddered, while up above the sky churned as thickly black as diesel exhaust. What further calamity might the mountain have in store, he wondered. In which torturous manner would he die?

Wilson began to shudder and moan from the agony of his burns when he heard the sound of crunching footsteps drawing near. He shifted and found Doug's ominous outline clarifying among the dark haze. A thin wind swirled the ash eastward just enough to accommodate some light, and then Wilson could see him clearly, the derelict looking like some wretched clay figure escaped from a kiln. Everything about him was gray, especially his hair which was coiffed up in grime. His clothes were in tatters. The exposed skin of his arms and neck and face was all charred and blistering.

Doug took several more steps and then loomed directly above Wilson. He was either smiling, or grimacing with pain, or both. A long moment of calculation passed between them as Wilson gazed up with morbid patience. He expected Doug to leave him where he lay. Or maybe even brain him with a sizzling hunk of the volcano.

"You look like you're trapped," Doug finally said.

Wilson awaited some clumsy coup de grâce.

"Tom? Can you hear me?"

"Yes. I'm trapped."

Doug surveyed the fallen tree as he gagged on the choking ash. "It's not so huge. I'll see if I can move it."

Wilson still thought it might be some kind of a ruse until the tree began to shift and slide down the back of his seared legs. The pain was astronomical, like a thousand bee stings every instant. Wilson shrieked and begged him to quit.

"Hang on," Doug said. "I've almost got it."

Doug squatted and lifted as much of the weight as he could manage. Even so, the bark and branches were scraping along Wilson's calves which caused him to howl and clench his fists and dig his toes into the ash. At last the tree thumped to the ground and Wilson's legs came free. Doug hunched over to hack out a dozen coughs that became laced with blood. Wilson rolled to his side and his right leg seemed to swing of its own accord. He slumped to the ground in despair. His femur had been fractured, and his knee was utterly demolished.

Doug had finally regained his breath and now he stared at his out-held hands, the skin peeled away and hanging from his fingers like the flesh of some rotten fruit. "My hands are garbage," he was saying. "My hands are garbage."

Wilson's truck lay bent and battered in the ditch. Even if the vehicle had been operative, the road was now intersected by hundreds, if not thousands, of fallen trees. That way was impossible, so Wilson and Doug agreed the best they could do for now was to relieve their burns in the creek. With great effort, Wilson was able to rise to one leg. He began hopping along with Doug's puzzling support, but it soon became apparent that the ash and debris made this mode of progress impossible as well. Doug went ahead with his ribboned hands flailing, and Wilson began to crawl.

It was a mere thirty yards to the creek, but the way was continually blockaded by an epic tangle of shorn and uprooted trees. The volcano had produced such an awesome lateral blast that even this many miles away only a handful of blackened firs remained standing in all the smoldering wasteland he could see. The air smelled like sulfur and the cinders of burnt fir needles.

Wilson kept pulling himself along, inch by agonizing inch. His movements were stirring up the ash so much that his windpipe kept clogging and he would stop and gasp for any air. Halfway along he reached a cluster of downed trees that had to be traversed, and it was only the most profound desperation that kept him going, for the pain of it all was beyond reckoning. As he began to crawl over yet another tree, the touch of his hand caused the bark to ignite in flame. He reeled back as sparks rose from the log like nature's black magic.

When at last Wilson reached the creek, he slithered down the bank and into the water like some broken lizard. What had only minutes before been a cold clear stream was now a lukewarm ooze the color and consistency of sewage. Though the water was not nearly as refreshing as Wilson had hoped, it did help to soothe his tormented skin. He arranged his body as comfortably as he could and then looked for Doug. Instead he spotted several elk fifty yards upstream that were also bathing their burnt hides. One of them was clearly dead. The others seemed well on their way. Wilson lay there in that riparian ruin watching endless debris floating past. Pumice, chunks of wood and trash, many dazed and floundering birds, a dead beaver. All the lifeless shards of the forest being conveyed in a muddy seep to sea.

Wilson began to hear Doug hollering at him from somewhere downstream. He wondered why he should even bother answering, but he finally shouted out his location. In a few moments Doug came gimping around the creekbend. He'd cleansed himself of much of the ash, and now his wounds showed all the starker. His forehead hung open as if it were some frowning second mouth. His arms looked like two limp sausages left to blacken and shrivel in the pan. And his hands were indeed garbage. He splashed down next to Wilson in a silty pool and gazed heavenward.

"Look at that," he said.

Half the sky was alive with sheets of red lightning that zapped and rinned through the ash plume, a continuous pyrotechnic display that could out-awe a thousand celebrations of independence.

"I can't believe it really blew," Doug said as the ground again shook and rumbled.

Wilson coughed out half a laugh. "What the hell did you expect was going to happen?"

"I don't know. Just didn't think it would be like this."

Neither the air nor the water was cold, but as they continued to bathe they each began to feel chilled. Soon enough their teeth were chattering, and then their whole bodies commenced to shake.

"What's happening to us?" Doug asked.

"We're going into shock."

"And what does that mean?"

"It means we won't last long if we just sit here."

Doug looked from Wilson to the outgoing flow of the stream. "This creek could be a way out. If we follow it down it'll lead us to the Toutle River and into town. You can float or crawl as far as you can, and I'll go ahead and get some help. I think that's our best shot."

Wilson was surprised to find himself in agreement. They decided to rest for a while and then try their luck with the creek. When they were ready, Doug stood and Wilson prepared himself for the grueling slog ahead. Then they heard a new sound, a growing rumble like that of an oncoming freight train. They shared a look of terror and began to instinctively claw back up the side of the bank, each of them stumbling and faltering in his own ragged fashion. And then it came growling around the corner, a turbulent mudflow unleashed by the mountain itself to remake the landscape as it gargled boulders and devoured whole stands of trees. Wilson and Doug were each bloodying themselves as they fought their way uphill, and it was by a margin of some few feet that they escaped the rush of the lahar as it snorted onward in steaming locomotion.

Afterwards they lay in the ash straining to breathe. Both of them were whimpering and fidgeting about in vain for a way to make the pain more bearable. Ash continued to dust them in their suffering, as though they were already inside that final crematorium. Both knew they could not endure.

"Of all the ways to die," Doug said. "There's no way we're getting out of here alive."

Wilson was not listening. He lay with his head in the crook of his arm envisioning Ellen and Maggie and his baby boy. So much joy that they would never share together. The years would pass and the memory of him would fade. Already he was fading.

"Tom?"

How fragile this shell keeping death at bay. And what manner of emptiness awaits on the other side? He scolded himself for his resignation, but the will to live was ebbing away with every excruciating wave of pain.

"Tom?"

"Mmm."

Doug gazed at him through his enflamed and ghoulish eyes. He too looked ready to die. "You were right. I did shoot them."

Wilson had no strength left for anger. If this was the world, he thought, then maybe it was best to leave.

"Since this is it, I thought you may as well know that you were right."

"How?" Wilson rasped. "How could you do it?"

"I wanted to save them from their suffering."

"You're a liar. You're a murderer and a liar. You did it for money somehow."

"Not for money. It was mercy."

"Mercy? Mercy?" Wilson repeated. "Who do you think you are? God? She might have gotten better. She might have been cured."

"Someday maybe. But not now." Doug paused to clear his windpipe and gather more breath. "Pops always said that he didn't want to grow old without Nana. He told me once that he couldn't bear to watch her lose her mind. To wither away like that. He talked about doing it himself. He showed me the gun he would use. But he couldn't do it. He wanted to, but he couldn't do it. So I helped him."

"He asked you to?"

Doug shook his head.

"Then you had no right. Even if he had asked, you had no right."

"I see that now. And I know I'm going to Hell for it."

"But you won't. You'll just die like everyone else. Without punishment. And Elmer will rot in prison for what you did."

"He's better off there than where he was."

Wilson wanted to cry, but there was no energy for that either. "Goddamnit. God damn you. I loved them so much. I loved them, and you took them away from the world, and now I have to die here next to you."

"I'm sorry, Tom."

"God damn you."

Doug tried to continue his confessional, but Wilson would not respond. And so they just shivered in the ash, waiting for their organs to fail. All was silence except the muted slurp of the mud below and an occasional fir cracking to fall amongst the others.

Wilson's pain was still intense, but the worst of it all was the chill that had frozen its way into his very bones. He would be happy enough to die now if only he could find some heat. A fire, an extra jacket. He'd give anything to have but a little warmth. Finally, he began to drift in and out of consciousness as feverish dreams blurred the line between real and unreal.

He imagined he was at home, in bed with the flu. Blankets were up to his chin, but he was still too cold for someone had left the ceiling fan on high. Around and around the fan blades rotated, but he was too sick and weak to stand and pull the string. Whomp. Whomp. The sound was maddening and growing louder. How he despised this chill. He must reach the fan. Must rise and make it stop. He was lifting himself, straining to grasp the fan's chain when he began to inhabit the actual world again and saw two dark-green military helicopters advancing above the other side of the creek.

Wilson waved pathetically and shouted out a long and hollow plea for rescue. The National Guard hueys passed and continued whirling down the valley. Wilson watched the helicopters recede until they had the sound and appearance of horseflies. Then he slumped back into the ash. Doug had made no effort to flag down the pilots.

"They can't see us," he said. "They're too high and we blend in too well."

Some minutes passed and then one of the helicopters could be heard returning. It flew on their side of the creek this time, much slower than before. With the last of his energy, Wilson removed his jacket and swung it over his head in weak circles. The helicopter drew near, paused, and made a tight hovering loop. Wilson watched the pilot point at them, and then the helicopter began to descend as its raucous blades churned up a flurry of ash. The skids made unsteady contact atop a balded knoll and two crewmen, one white and one black, jumped out and came tromping over.

"Let's get the hell out of here," the white crewman shouted.

"I can't walk," Wilson said.

"What?"

"I said, I can't walk."

The black crewman was as tall and powerful as a heavyweight prize-fighter, but even so Wilson was astounded to find himself scooped up and carried over the man's shoulder. As they were heading back to the helicopter, he watched Doug scuffle with the other crewman.

"I want to stay, I want to stay," Doug was screaming.

"You're okay now," the crewman hollered. "Stop fighting me. You're going to be okay."

"Let me die here."

"Murph. Hey, Murph," the white crewman called. "This one's delirious. Find those restraints for me, will ya?"

When everyone was loaded, the helicopter lifted and buzzed down the valley. Doug had been strapped to his seat and he was glowering at the crewmen who were vigilantly searching for more survivors. Wilson looked like he'd been exhumed and resurrected and was dying once more.

His vision kept dissolving into a blizzard of white, and between cycles of blindness he saw that the black crewman had leaned toward him to ask how he was faring.

"Water," Wilson muttered.

The crewman helped him to take a few sips and then pointed out the window. "You oughta see what almost got you."

Mount St. Helens had been decapitated, and from its jagged neck bloomed a deathly gray cauliflower of ash and gas and pulverized rock. The stalk now stood twelve miles high and it was flickering with streaks of blue and purple lighting. A slight wind had commenced to scatter the ash-plume east, and the fallout was already darkening distant lands with what would soon become fertile new soil. To the north, Spirit Lake had been buried under two hundred feet of debris and then refilled with superheated pyroclastic sludge that simmered like the broth of a new beginning. Beyond this so many trees lay in immense comb strokes that all of Portland and Seattle could be burnt and rebuilt and still there'd be timber left to spare. Overall, this previously green paradise now stretched mile after drab gray mile in monochromatic destruction, the only color provided by the occasional small fire.

The helicopter banked and the pilot picked up the Toutle River which was galloping at double-speed and looked like a flood of wet cement. The astonished crewmen pointed out homes that had been ripped from their foundations forty miles from the mountain and become newly mobile. There were barns and garages and livestock racing along, tractors and bulldozers and logging trucks drifting sideways or upside down. Two crazed horses were straining to stay afloat and they watched as one of them disappeared, resurfaced, and then vanished for good. Throughout the river, hundreds of salmon were constantly leaping in silvery flashes to escape the now scalding water, and as they approached the Cowlitz, a bridge became so overwhelmed by a logjam that it finally snapped and swiveled and flowed along like a surfboard with the rest of that unlikely flotsam.

"I never thought I'd see something so crazy as this," the black crewman said. He turned toward Wilson and saw that he had slumped over and nearly fallen out of his chair. "Hey, buddy? Hey? Oh, man. Don't go on us. Hey, buddy? Hey—"

Wilson awoke as though he'd been lost to time. He shifted some and looked around the small hospital room in which he lay alone. Ash tumbled outside the window like the devil's snow.

He tried to sit up in the bed so that he could inspect his burns and his movements pulled an IV loose. The station monitor flat lined with an obnoxious blare and in a few moments a young intern nurse came running into the room. She seemed surprised that he was still alive.

Quickly and wordlessly she reinserted the IV. Then she picked up a large needle from the cart. Wilson was recoiling from the shot she intended to administer when a husky voice in the doorway instructed her to stop. The intern set the needle down and backed away as the doctor stepped forward. He was an elderly man with bushy eyebrows and a Roman nose.

"How are you feeling, Tom?" the doctor asked.

Wilson had not quite taken stock of himself yet so he rocked from side to side and tested his leg. "I feel sore," he said. "But I'm not in agony like I was."

"That's very good," the doctor said. He pulled out a chair and dragged it next to Wilson's bed. "Do you know where you are right now?"

"I think I'm in St. John's Hospital."

"That's right. And do you know what day it is?"

"Monday?"

The doctor chuckled. "Not quite."

"I guess it must be Tuesday then."

"No. It's not Tuesday either. It's Sunday."

Wilson frowned with disbelief. "I've been asleep for a week?"

"Yes. We've been holding you in a drug-induced coma. And you'd still be in one were it not for . . ." He aimed an arching eyebrow at the intern.

"I'd like to see my wife," Wilson said.

"Of course. Very soon. And I'll make you a deal. I won't put you back under as long as you promise to do everything I ask of you in regards to your skin. It's very important that we continue to scrape away all the dead skin so that we can limit your risk of infection. Just understand that the process can be extremely painful."

"I'll do anything it takes as long as I can see my wife and kids."

"Very good. That will be our bargain."

The doctor went on to elaborate in great detail the treatments, surgeries, procedures and timelines by which Wilson would hopefully regain his strength and mobility. When he was finished, he patted Wilson on the arm.

"You're a very lucky man," he said.

"I don't feel so lucky."

"You will."

The doctor stood and moved for the door.

"Doctor," Wilson said.

"Yes?"

"Could you make a phone call for me?"

"I'll notify your wife immediately."

"Doctor, I need you to call Detective Depp. He works for the Clark County Sheriff's Department. I need you to tell him to come visit me as soon as possible."

"I'll see what I can do. Now it's very important that you rest."

"I will. But Doctor . . . I really need you to make that call."

S ummer had gotten off to a sweltering start. Ellen and the children waited atop the hot noon asphalt as Wilson fought his way out of their new station wagon. His crutches came first, next the good leg, and then he grunted and lifted and arrived at a swinging upright. Despite the heat, Wilson wore long sleeves and a baseball hat to hide the worst of his burn scars.

Maggie was giggling. "Daddy is *so* slow."

"Hey," Ellen said. "Don't make fun of Daddy. He's still recuperating."

"What's recupating?"

"It means that his owies are getting better."

"But why does it take so long?"

"Because Daddy had some very bad owies."

"Oh."

Ellen shifted the baby to the other arm, took hold of Maggie's hand, and began heading toward the entrance of the nursing home as Wilson crutched after.

Inside the lobby, the receptionist beamed as she saw them all approaching. "You sure weren't exaggerating when you said you'd be here every day."

"At least until I get back to work," Wilson replied.

"Would you like to see her in her room, or shall I ask her to come down?"

"Her room is fine."

They took the elevator to the second floor and then walked down a carpeted hallway that appeared very much like a modern hotel. Halfway along they stopped and knocked. In a moment, the door swung open. Louanne clapped her hands with great cheer.

"Tom! Ellen! It's so nice of you to stop by." She noticed the crutches. "Oh dear. What happened to your leg?"

For the fifth time, Wilson explained how he had fallen from a ladder.

Louanne tsked and shook her head toward Ellen. "You need to make sure that he's a lot more careful next time."

"Oh. I'm pretty confident there won't be a next time," Ellen said.

"Well, I certainly hope not."

Louanne looked at the baby with some confusion, and then led them inside as she commenced yet another brief tour of the room. Her studio was quite small, but it seemed comfortable enough. The one window looked out onto a bright flowery courtyard. Paintings of pastoral landscapes hung about the walls. The bookshelf was full of romance novels and there was space on the table for her puzzles and sewing machine.

"I'll only be here for a few more days," she explained. "Just until Lesley gets back from his big fishing trip."

Wilson looked to the floor.

"Well, it's a very nice room," Ellen said. "I'm sure you'll be happy here for as long as he's away."

"Oh sure. Just a little bit lonely without him is all."

They made small talk for a while longer, and then Wilson announced that they'd better be heading up toward the mountain before it got too late.

"Mount St. Helens!" Louanne exclaimed. "How wonderful. You know, you're always welcome to stay at our cabin."

"That's very kind of you," Wilson said.

"It's not the most glamorous place. But it sure is beautiful out there."

"Yeah. Well, it was great to see you, Louanne."

"Oh. It was so nice of you all to stop by. Will you come visit again soon?"

Wilson nodded. "We sure will."

In Castle Rock they stopped for gas and a quick lunch. Then they continued east on what remained of Spirit Lake Highway. They were perhaps fifteen miles from the mountain when they pulled over and walked out to the edge of a sweeping viewpoint.

Mount St. Helens looked like some broken crown unfit for any king. Spirit Lake was nothing but a scummy clog of timber. To the north and west the land sprawled for miles like the surface of the moon. Ellen began to cry.

"I didn't think it would be so hard for me to come here," she said.

"It's definitely sad to see how much of it is gone."

"It's not that. It's being here and knowing that you could be dead right now."

He took her gently by the shoulders. "But I'm not. I'm right here with you."

"Don't you ever put yourself in harm's way like that again. You hear me?"

"I hear you. If there's anything I've learned from this whole experience, it's that I only get so many days to love you . . ."

She leaned back so that she could look into his eyes.

". . . And I'm determined to make the most of them."

Ellen wiped the tears and mascara from her cheeks and managed a smile. "Listen to us. We sound like we should be in a movie."

"Who would play me?"

"I don't know. Someone crazy."

Maggie began hollering for them to come look.

"What is it, honey?" Ellen asked.

"There's deer!" she shouted.

Far below, in a former creek now silted over, they watched a small herd of elk picking their way through the ash in search of something, anything, to eat. Wilson watched them continue on in what seemed like a futile pursuit when a big cow slowed, sniffed, and began to root up a fresh bloom of fireweed. Others soon joined.

"Well, I'll be damned," Wilson said. "They're already coming back."

"Would you like us to try and get closer?" Ellen asked.

"No. No, I think this is close enough for me."

They were all heading back toward the station wagon when Wilson noticed a portly middle-aged man and his teenage daughter clamber out of a truck bearing an Iowa license plate. Almost immediately the man began snapping photographs, his daughter following him around in astonishment. Wilson watched them with curiosity, and then humor, for the man was mostly aiming his camera at the wrong side of the road.

"Look at the destruction," the man was saying. "My God. Just look at what the mountain did to this forest."

Wilson began crutching in their direction. "Excuse me, folks."

The man and his daughter turned to him in synchrony.

"I couldn't help but notice you over here taking your pictures," Wilson said. "And I just thought I'd tell you that this patch of forest wasn't knocked down by the explosion."

"No?" the man said.

"No. This is a clearcut. This is what it generally looks like after all the trees have been logged off."

The man turned and saw the forest anew. He began to chuckle. "I guess it's apparent that we're not from around here, huh?"

"Well, I gathered that much from your license plate."

The girl began tugging on her father's shirt and whispered a few words that Wilson could not catch. As she spoke, the man began looking at Wilson with heightened interest, taking stock of his crutches and his scars.

Wilson grew uncomfortable. He began to backpedal.

"Say," the man called. "Say, didn't we see you on the television?"

"Enjoy your trip," Wilson said as he turned and crutched away.

"I think that was him," the man said.

Ellen had been watching the entire episode. She smiled with some sympathy as Wilson returned.

"You're gonna have to get used to it eventually," she said.

"Maybe one day when I'm old and gray." He shook his head. "Nah. Probably not even then."

"Are you ready to go home?" she asked.

"Yeah. Let's go home."

Wilson leaned against the rails of the newly constructed pigpen. He watched the hogman toss another bucket of mash, and a dozen pigs grunted and oinked and jostled for their rightful share. The hogman set down his bucket and folded his arms across his chest.

"It don't ever get old for me. I just love to watch these pigs doing their thing."

"I'd say you were lucky to have found your vocation," Wilson said.

"Luck didn't have nothing to do with it. I just kept trying on hats until I found one that fit. You were the lucky one. You got it right on the first try."

"Well, when you put it like that . . ." Wilson stepped back from the pigpen and made an effort to bend his bad leg so that it rested on the bottom rail.

The hogman had been watching him. "How's the rehabilitation coming along?"

"Oh. Slow and steady."

"Your burns don't look so bad anymore. Little leathery, but you're still a heck of a lot better looking than me."

Wilson chuckled. "Yeah, it's the leg that really gives me grief."

"What you gonna do if someone tries to run on you?"

"Figure I'll just shoot the first two or three and let my reputation precede me from there."

"Don't sound like protocol to me. But I could get behind that."

Wilson turned and gazed across the autumnal valley that was scented with woodsmoke and fresh rain. Stormclouds were running for the mountains, and the long lost sun had finally returned to luster that evergreen landscape. To the north, the clouds had cleared just enough to provide a glimpse of Mount St. Helens, its summit flat from this angle, and diminished by more than a thousand feet. The hogman had nearly lost his view of it altogether.

The hogman nodded in the mountain's direction. "That big old gal there showed you just how mortal you are, didn't she?"

"What do you mean? I always knew that I was mortal."

"No, you didn't. Not really."

Wilson smiled. "You're getting awfully wise in your old age. What's the secret?"

The hogman didn't even have to consider the question. "Sunshine, hard work, and lots of bacon."

"You know, Gene. Some of these experts are saying that bacon's bad for your health. Clogs up the arteries or something."

"And which experts are they? Bunch of vegetarians? I don't trust nobody that would willingly trade bacon for tofu." The hogman reached over the top rail and shook Wilson's hand. "Got a surprise for you in the shop."

"What's that?"

"Go on and see for yourself."

"They're ready already?"

"Wrapped and ready already. Got your name written all over the boxes so it won't be hard to tell which are yours."

"You're on your game."

"Got to be. This franchise is expanding. Speaking of which, you sure must have a growing family. Two whole pigs amounts to a lot of eating."

Wilson stepped back off the rail. "One of them's not for me."

D usk was settling over the land when Wilson pulled up to the ramshackle property so many others avoided like a plague. He shut off his engine, unloaded two boxes of meat, and walked with a slight limp up to the moldering trailer.

Wilson was struggling to backhand a knock when the door swung out and nearly pushed him off the tiny porch.

"Damnit, Elmer. I've got a whole armload of stuff here."

"I'm sorry about that," Elmer said in his nasally way. "I'm still not quite used to having this door yet."

The trailer was never going to be a charming place, but at least now it didn't seem like such a shop of horror. Wilson had helped him haul in some decent second-hand furniture, and the pantry contained items which actually appeared edible. Elmer himself looked almost respectable in the stiff new clothes he'd been able to afford, and his teeth were being repaired on a charitable installment plan.

Wilson followed him into the rear of the trailer where Elmer opened up the chest freezer he'd recently finagled from a neighbor. As Wilson lowered the boxes inside, Elmer bent over and beheld his new abundance with the amazement of a lifelong pauper.

"All that there is really meat?"

"I'd say it'll see you through the winter. What do you think?"

"Gosh. It'd take about a thousand rats to fill those boxes up."

Wilson wagged his finger. "No more rats. In fact, no more rodents of any kind. Never again."

"Are you sure I can't give you some money for all this?"

"Like I said, you should be saving your money so that you can buy yourself a decent trailer."

"Well, can I at least cook you up a pork chop or something?"

"Nah. I've gotta get to the office and finish up some reports."

Elmer followed him outside. He stood at the edge of the porch watching Wilson as he began taking the path back to his cruiser.

"Hey, Deputy Wilson?"

He stopped and turned.

"I was just wondering. Well . . . How come you're always so kind to me?"

"Don't worry about it."

"I mean, it ain't like it's part of your job. Why do you even bother helping a nobody like me?"

Wilson thought about it for a moment. "Because I can, Elmer. Because being a deputy means that I get to."

"I sure wish there was a lot more cops like you in this world. I wish they were all as decent as you."

"Don't say that, Elmer. There's plenty of us. More than you know."

And with that Wilson turned and headed for his cruiser. He'd just gotten to his car when a team of geese began honking loudly overhead. He paused for a moment to watch them traveling south, a shifting V against the darkening sky. Then he slid in behind the wheel of his cruiser, started the engine, and drove on down the quiet country road, ready for whoever might need him next.

Acknowledgments

This relatively short book owes its existence to a great many people. I must first thank its chief inspirers, my brother Tim and father Vern, talented raconteurs and two of the toughest and biggest-hearted police officers southwest Washington has been lucky enough to claim.

Thank you, Andrew Hamilton, another dedicated law enforcement officer, for a lifetime of love and support. And thanks to the Longview and Kelso Police Departments and the Clark and Cowlitz County Sheriffs' Departments for allowing me to ride along with them so often, and for always keeping me safe and entertained.

My research for this book was greatly enhanced by the congenial staff at the Longview Public Library, and by the generosity of local historian Margaret Colf Hepola who was still sharp and vivacious at the age of 97.

Books that contributed to the creation of my own include Steve Olson's *Eruption*, William Boly's *Fire Mountain*, and Richard Waitt's *In the Path of Destruction*. I especially owe a debt of gratitude to the Longview *Daily News* staff who covered the buildup to the eruption and other local happenings from 1979 to 1980.

Many thanks to fellow wordsmiths James LeMonds, Michael Gurian, Spike Walker, Charles Johnson and Craig Anderson for encouraging me to keep writing and then showing me how to do it more skillfully. I wish them all everlasting energy and inspiration.

To my early readers, your insights, suggestions, flattery, and occasional ridicule were essential. Thank you, Ira Amstadter, Michael Amstadter, Susan Amstadter, Bob Ferris, Karen Gandy, Carol Hamilton, Scott Hourigan, Brandon Krebs, Boone Mora, Shawn Nyman, Rich Proszek, Danielle Riggs, Judy Romano, Larry Wasserman and whoever else I may be forgetting. You are all hired for my next book.

I'm lucky enough to have a day job that I actually like, and better yet, a boss that I admire. Erik, thanks for your flexibility, camaraderie, and largesse. Let's keep saving the world.

My hat's off to Andrew Juarez, Russ Davis and the Gray Dog Press team for their stunning book design. The old adage is not to judge a book by its cover, and thankfully these talented designers understand better than most that that's a bunch of malarkey.

Logan Amstadter, somehow I think you're both the unstoppable force and the immovable object. You manage to keep me grounded even while we're dashing around the globe. Thank you for reminding me that I don't aspire to be merely a writer, but an artist as well. Your support has been incalculable and your partnership is my greatest blessing. I can't wait for you to be my bride.

And finally, this book is in memory of Jeri Gosch. It took me a decade, but I think I finally got it right this time.

CPSIA information can be obtained
at www.ICGtesting.com
Printed in the USA
LVHW041534141119
637372LV00002B/341